Runaway horse . . .

Pirate blazed past the finish wire a length ahead of the mare.

"All right, Pirate!" Melanie cheered.

Suddenly there was a gasp from the crowd. Melanie looked for Pirate and felt her heart begin to pound. The horse wasn't slowing. He was still going hard toward the next turn. The mare was running beside Pirate, on his outside. It seemed as though the two horses thought the race wasn't over yet.

"What's the matter?" Melanie asked. "Why aren't they stopping?"

Then Pirate lunged and slammed into the mare's shoulder. The mare fell as Pirate rammed her. Pirate kept going toward the outside rail and crashed right through it. Naomi, the jockey, fell hard on the other side of the fence. Even from as far away as she was, Melanie could see the flash of blood, bright red against Pirate's deep black chest.

THOROUGHBRED

MELANIE'S TREASURE

CREATED BY
JOANNA CAMPBELL

WRITTEN BY
ALLISON ESTES

HarperPaperbacks
A Division of HarperCollins*Publishers*

HarperPaperbacks
A Division of HarperCollins*Publishers*
10 East 53rd Street, New York, N.Y. 10022-5299

ISBN 0-06-106798-9

HarperCollins®, 🏭 ®, and HarperPaperbacks™ are trademarks of HarperCollins*Publishers* Inc.

Cover art: © 1998 Daniel Weiss Associates, Inc.

First printing: April 1998

Printed in the United States of America

Visit HarperPaperbacks on the World Wide Web at
http://www.harpercollins.com

❖ 10 9 8 7 6 5 4 3 2 1

MELANIE'S TREASURE

1

SHE COULDN'T REMEMBER EXACTLY HOW SHE FIRST CAME UP with the idea. But twelve-year-old Melanie Graham was sure of one thing: It was the greatest plan she had ever had and she was going to carry it out.

That morning at school, Melanie sat jiggling one knee impatiently while she waited for her best friend, Aynslee Harland, to show up. Melanie couldn't wait to tell Aynslee about her awesome plan. In fact, she was counting on Aynslee to be in on it with her. She was sure she would never try it alone. Assembly had already started when Aynslee finally slipped into the seat Melanie had saved for her. "Rad hair, Mel," Aynslee whispered appreciatively, eyeing the bright blue streaks in Melanie's white-blond hair.

"Thanks!" Melanie whispered back, tugging at the navy blue skirt of her school uniform to straighten it.

Melanie hated wearing the uniform. She hated doing anything the same way everyone else was doing it. But she had decided that if she had to dress like everyone else, at least she could make sure her hair displayed her uniqueness. So she kept it short in the back and over her ears but longer on top. And every couple of weeks she dyed different colored streaks into the long parts with Kool-Aid. This week the streaks were blue.

She brushed a strand of blue hair out of her brown eyes and leaned toward Aynslee, cupping a hand around her mouth. "Ayns," Melanie whispered. "I have such a cool idea." She grinned at Aynslee, who peered at her with her serious blue-gray eyes and raised an eyebrow expectantly.

Melanie wasn't close to many people. She didn't have a lot of friends, and most of the time she preferred to be alone. She was known for saying exactly what was on her mind, which made other kids uneasy around her. But not Aynslee. Aynslee wasn't afraid of anything or anybody. Melanie admired that. Also, Melanie had something in common with Aynslee that none of the other kids would ever understand. Melanie lived alone with her dad because her mother had died when she was little. Aynslee lived with her father and stepmother because Aynslee's mother had moved out years before. Melanie had a hard time talking about her mom to anybody except Aynslee.

"Melanie, if you have something important to say, please raise your hand and I will invite you to share it with all of us," Mr. Howard, the headmaster, said. "Otherwise, be quiet." He gave her a stern look.

Melanie sighed. She was tempted to raise her hand and ask a smart-aleck question, but she made herself keep still. In less than two weeks, she would be finished with the seventh grade at Abraham Lincoln Middle School. Then she could put away the hated school uniforms for the whole summer.

A few times that year Melanie had gotten into trouble at school, mostly with Aynslee, who was talented at coming up with ways to test Mr. Howard. They had never done anything really bad. Mostly it was stuff that Melanie thought was harmless and funny—like the time they had glued the main outside doors shut, or the time they had stolen all the chalk and hidden it so that none of the teachers could write on the boards.

But of course Mr. Howard hadn't thought any of it was funny. Melanie had been warned that if she caused any more trouble at school she would be given a research paper to do over the summer. The last thing Melanie wanted was to spend the summer writing a paper. She was going to spend every day of her summer vacation riding horses at Clarebrook Stables. Her dad had promised her that if she did all her homework and stayed out of trouble at school, she could lease her favorite horse for the summer. So when Mr. Howard scolded her, she gave Aynslee a promising look and contented herself with sketching a picture of two horses and riders on a hill with a big full moon shining down on them. She folded the picture and passed it to Aynslee, who gave her a questioning look but kept quiet.

It wasn't until lunch that she finally had time to tell Aynslee what she was planning. Melanie plunked her tray down on the table and sat down in front of it. Then she turned to face Aynslee.

"Okay, let's hear it," Aynslee said, swallowing a bite of vegetable lasagna. She tucked her straight dark hair behind her ears and peered at Melanie.

"Okay," Melanie said. "You know next Monday is Memorial Day, right?"

Aynslee nodded. "So?"

"So it'll be slow at Clarebrook because everybody leaves the city for the holiday weekend." Clarebrook was the oldest stable in New York City. Melanie and Aynslee both took riding lessons there.

"So?" Aynslee said again. She took another bite of her lasagna.

Melanie watched her for a moment. Aynslee's eyes were half closed, a signal that she was already bored. Melanie hurriedly got the rest of it out.

"So the barn closes early on Sunday. Nobody will be around except Red." Melanie grinned. "And I checked the calendar. There's a full moon."

Aynslee's bored expression was quickly replaced by a look of keen interest. "Are you thinking what I'm thinking?" Aynslee asked.

Melanie nodded. "Moonlight ride!" she and Aynslee said at the same time.

4

"We can go off the bridle path and no one will care," Melanie said excitedly.

"We can go anywhere we want," Aynslee said. "We can gallop around the Great Lawn!" Then she frowned. "But what about Red? And Tiger?"

Red was the old man who had been the night watchman at Clarebrook for many years. Tiger was his dog—an ugly mix of shepherd, hound, and pit bull. Together the two of them prowled the stables at night, making sure the horses were fine and guarding against intruders.

"I got it all figured out," Melanie said, and she whispered the rest of her plan to Aynslee, who listened carefully, nibbling at her lasagna.

"Mel," Aynslee said when she had heard the whole plan, "you're a genius. Skin me." Aynslee held out her hand and Melanie swiped it with her own down-turned palm, grinning broadly.

"So can you get out of the house Sunday night?" Melanie asked.

"No problem. The parents have tickets to the symphony," Aynslee said, putting on a fake English accent. "What about you?"

"What—are you kidding? You know my dad's never home." Melanie's father, Will Graham, owned a huge recording studio. He was always busy listening to new bands or having dinner with clients. "Angela will be there, but by six o'clock she'll be glued to the television," Melanie said. "I could probably set off an explosion next to her and she wouldn't notice."

The hardest part after that was waiting for the week to end. When Sunday night finally rolled around, Melanie had a scare. Her father was supposed to be going out, but at the last minute his plans were canceled. She knew because she had been eavesdropping outside his study and heard his end of the phone conversation.

Melanie stood in the hall, chewing nervously on her pinky. She had counted on her dad being out for the evening. He wouldn't let her out alone after dark. She was supposed to be at Clarebrook at seven-thirty. Aynslee would never let her hear the end of it if she didn't show up.

She debated whether to tell her dad she was sleeping over at Aynslee's. But a couple of times she'd gotten caught using that excuse to go somewhere she wasn't supposed to be. Now her dad wasn't easy to fool. He'd call Aynslee's house to check up on her, or make sure Angela, the housekeeper, did. And when he called, Melanie knew, she had better be there. Really, though, she didn't like to stay at Aynslee's house. She had always been a light sleeper and could never rest in a strange bed.

While she was trying to decide what to do, she heard the creak of her father's leather chair as he stood up. Melanie hurried into the study so that he wouldn't catch her skulking around outside and know she had been listening to his phone conversations.

"Hey, Mel," Will Graham said to his daughter.

"Hi, Dad," Melanie said, going to give him a hug. She hadn't seen him since the night before. He'd gone out to hear some band before she went to sleep and had left for a breakfast meeting early in the morning before she woke up. She hugged him hard, breathing in the familiar smell of his starched shirt and his cologne. Then she pressed her ear against his chest and listened to the reassuring thudding of his heart. It was an old habit of hers, though when she had begun it she couldn't say—maybe it was when her mother died. Melanie was always listening for things. The familiar hum of the refrigerator kicking on, the whizzing of car tires on the wet streets when it rained, and the annoying racket of the garbage trucks in the morning were sounds that told her everything was normal. The world was working okay.

"How's my blue-haired girl?" Will Graham said affectionately, giving her a kiss on the head. Then he held her at arm's length, looking her over with a mock-serious expression. "I think it's high time we took you to the tattoo parlor, don't you?"

"Da-ad," Melanie protested. "Tattoos are gross! You can never get rid of them. The Kool-Aid washes out after a couple of weeks."

"Did you do your homework?" he asked her.

"Yes," Melanie said. "But tomorrow's Memorial Day, remember? There's no school."

"Oh. Right. I forgot." He frowned slightly and quickly ran his fingers through his long, graying hair.

Melanie knew people thought her dad was handsome. She did, too. He was tall and muscular and tan, and always dressed in expensive suits. Melanie was slight and thin, with dainty features in her elfin face. Her dad said that Melanie looked just like her mother, especially her eyes. Melanie's eyes were dark brown, with a slight downward tilt at the corners that made her look a little sad.

"Aren't you going out?" Melanie asked her father. She was careful to keep her voice sounding neutral.

"I was supposed to," he said with a sigh.

"Was it a date?" Melanie asked.

"No, dinner with a client."

"Oh." Melanie thought a minute. "Well, why don't you call Susan and ask her to have dinner with you?"

Susan was the woman her dad had been seeing for the past couple of months. Out of all the women he had dated over the years, she liked Susan best, although she would never let her dad know.

He gave her a disbelieving look. "I thought you didn't like Susan."

Melanie shrugged. "She's all right. I just thought since your business dinner was canceled you might like to make other plans."

"Well, Susan's out of town this weekend. But thank you for your consideration," he said with a skeptical smile.

"You're welcome," she said. Inside, though, she was beginning to really worry. How was she going to get to

Clarebrook by seven-thirty with her dad hanging around? Then she had one more thought. "You should go to the gym." She and her dad had a membership in the huge brand-new gym on Columbus Avenue. "They got the new rock-climbing wall finished," she added.

Will Graham's face registered interest. "You know, I might just do that, Mel. I've been meaning to try it out. Want to come?" he asked.

Melanie shook her head. "I'm kind of tired. I think I'm going to finish my book report, then just go to bed early. You go on, though," she urged.

"Hey, Mel, you've really been doing great with the schoolwork," he said approvingly. "Two more weeks and that horse is as good as yours." He winked at her, then frowned, looking perplexed. "What's his name? Candy Bar? Jelly Bean?"

"Milky Way," Melanie told him.

"Oh right, Milky Way. Anyway, keep up the good work," he said, smiling.

"I will," Melanie promised. "So, are you going to the gym or what?"

"Are you trying to get rid of me?" Will Graham said to his daughter, pretending to look suspicious.

"Yep," Melanie said cheerfully. "I'm not used to you being home for more than half an hour every day. It throws me off."

"Well, I guess I'll go climb some rocks then," he said, and got up to go change.

Melanie went to her room and sat down at her desk.

She took out her sketchbook and an ebony pencil and began working on a picture of Milky Way that she'd started. In a few minutes, her dad stuck his head in the door. "I'm leaving, Mel," he reported.

Melanie glanced at the clock on her desk. It was seven fifteen. She would have just enough time to make it to the barn. "Okay, Dad," she said, pretending to be too busy to look up.

"See you later," her father said.

"Bye, Dad."

A few seconds later, Melanie heard the front door close. She turned on her computer and closed the door of her room. Then she hurried downstairs. Angela was in the kitchen, ironing and watching the tiny television mounted under one of the cabinets. Melanie went to the refrigerator and took out an apple and a bag of baby carrots. "I'm going to be working on my computer for a while, Angela," she told the housekeeper. Angela nodded, sliding the iron expertly over the shirt.

Melanie found her paddock boots by the kitchen door and picked them up, hiding them behind her back as she sidled out of the kitchen. Angela never even looked at her. Melanie felt her heart begin to race with excitement. In half an hour it would be dark—and she and Aynslee would be riding in Central Park! Melanie laced her paddock boots, grabbed her jacket and the carrots and apple, and slipped out the front door, closing it soundlessly behind her.

2

THREE BLOCKS UP AND TWO BLOCKS OVER, MELANIE CAUGHT sight of the old brick building that was Clarebrook Stables. She hurried down the last half of the block but then slowed when she didn't see Aynslee. She didn't want anyone to notice her hanging around outside the stables. There was a parking garage next door. The attendant wasn't around, so she ducked inside to wait for Aynslee to show up.

Melanie was peering down the block, anxiously watching for Aynslee, when someone grabbed her from behind. Melanie nearly jumped out of her skin. She whirled around and recognized Aynslee's pale face. "Ha, ha!" Aynslee cackled. "Gotcha!"

"What are you trying to do—give me a heart attack?" Melanie said.

"You just never learn, do you, Mel?" Aynslee said with an exaggerated heavy sigh.

"You know I hate it when you sneak up on me like that." Melanie was annoyed at Aynslee for ambushing her and at herself for being startled. She should have expected it.

"Oh come on," Aynslee said. "You're such a baby sometimes."

Melanie regarded her friend for a moment. The thought crossed her mind that Aynslee didn't really have all the qualifications that a best friend ought to have. Besides being older than Melanie because she'd been held back a year in school, Aynslee was unpredictable and hard to please. It could be exhausting being friends with her. And sometimes she could be downright mean.

"I believe we have a moonlight ride on our agenda for the evening?" Aynslee said coolly in her fake English accent. "Are you coming?"

Melanie stepped toward her friend. Well, they did have fun together. Aynslee put her arm around Melanie's shoulders and the two girls walked out of the garage laughing.

"You got the pizza?" Melanie asked. They were going to have to figure out a way to get Red, the night watchman, to let them into the barn. Melanie had suggested bribing him with pizza.

"Yep," Aynslee said. She slipped her backpack off one shoulder and unzipped it, then took out a greasy paper bag.

"Do you think two slices is enough?" Melanie asked. "Maybe we should have gotten him a whole pie."

Aynslee shrugged "He's just one guy. How much can one old dude eat?"

"What about Tiger?" Melanie asked. They also had to get past Red's dog, who had a reputation for being vicious. Aynslee had thought of bringing some meat to feed to the dog in case he was loose when they came into the stables.

Aynslee patted a lump in the pocket of her jacket. "All taken care of," she said smugly.

There was a big garage door at the front of the building where the horses went in and out, but it was closed. With a glance around to be sure no one was watching them, the two girls went up the rusty, wrought-iron steps that led to the smaller office door of Clarebrook. Melanie cupped her hands around the sides of her face and tried peering through the smudged window.

"I don't see Red in there," she reported.

"Knock," Aynslee said.

Melanie rapped on the door a few times. There was no response. "Do you think he's asleep?" she asked.

Just then, with a lurch and a groan, the big front door began to open. Melanie jumped again.

Aynslee gave her an amused look. "Man, are you jumpy. Settle down, will you?"

The door opened about chest high, and Red, the night watchman, ducked under it, pushing a wheelbarrow with a shovel and a broom laid across it. He was going out to clean whatever manure was left on the streets from the horses that had been ridden to the park that day.

Aynslee came down the steps and stood in front of the man. "Hi, Red," she said with a charming smile.

"Well, hey there, Aynslee," Red replied. Melanie knew he had worked at Clarebrook for most of his adult life. His hair was beginning to gray, and he wore a pair of old-fashioned wire-rimmed glasses that gave him a studious look, in spite of his grubby blue coveralls. "Hey, Melanie. What brings you girls out here this evening?" He sounded genuinely glad to see them, and Melanie felt a second of regret. She hoped Red didn't get in trouble for what they were about to do.

"Red, we left something in our locker this morning. I know the barn is supposed to be closed, but we really need it. Do you think we could just go in and get it? It's really important. Right, Mel?" Aynslee said, stepping meaningfully on Melanie's foot.

Melanie pulled her foot away, wincing. "Um, yeah," she added. "It's . . . homework."

"Mmm-hmm. Homework. That is important," Red said. "Well, I'm just goin' out to do the street. Can you go on in and get what you need and then get out under the door here?"

"Sure, Red. Hey, by the way, we brought you some pizza. We heard you liked olives and anchovies," Aynslee said, holding out the bag to him.

14

"Olives and anchovies—why that's my favorite," Red said. "Thank you! I tell you what—just leave it on the mounting block in there and I'll get it when I come back. That's mighty thoughtful of you girls."

"No problem, Red," Aynslee said.

"Thanks for letting us in," Melanie added.

"And listen," Red said. "Don't go into the office, you hear? I put ol' Tiger in there while I'm out and he wouldn't like it if anybody went in there. You know what I mean? He's not too friendly with folks."

"Okay, Red. We won't," the girls assured him.

He lifted the arms of the wheelbarrow and started down the street. The girls watched him stop at the corner and scoop up a pile of manure. Then he rounded the turn and headed up the avenue out of sight.

"Let's do it," Aynslee said. "If we time this just right, we'll be out the door before he gets back around. This is going to be easier than I thought," she added, ducking under the half-closed door.

Inside the building, Melanie paused for a moment and looked around the tiny deserted ring. She'd been taking lessons at Clarebrook since she was ten, but she had never stopped being slightly amazed at the place. It was over a hundred years old, and looked it. On the main floor was the riding arena and the office. There were ramps leading to the floors above and below where the horses were stabled. Long ago, Clarebrook had been a livery stable. Once Melanie had snuck up to the top floor and found several old carriages and sleighs still stored there, their velvet seats covered with a thick layer of dust.

"Come on. We haven't got much time." Aynslee was pulling her by the arm toward the office.

"But Red said not to go in there. Tiger's in there," Melanie reminded her.

"That's the whole point," Aynslee said. "We have to make sure Tiger's not running around loose when we get back."

"But maybe he won't be," Melanie protested. "Let's just let him alone. He won't bother us once we're on the horses, anyway," Melanie pointed out.

"You ever see Tiger act friendly to anybody?" Aynslee asked.

Melanie shook her head. In fact, once she had walked by the barn when it was closed and had stopped to peek in the window of the big front door. Tiger must have sensed her there, because as she pressed her face against the window, Tiger jumped up against the glass from the other side. For a moment Melanie's face was an inch from the dog's mottled brown-and-white muzzle, fangs bared, snarling ferociously. Melanie had jumped back so fast that she fell down on the sidewalk. Her heart still skipped a beat when she remembered it.

Aynslee cautiously opened the door of the office just enough to see Tiger's yellowish eyes glaring at her. She quickly took a small foil package out of her pocket and unwrapped it. In it was a small ball of cooked hamburger.

"How is that going to keep him away from us if he's out when we get back?" Melanie asked.

Aynslee took the ball of hamburger and chucked it into the office. "Good night, Tiger," she said. "Have a nice nap." She crumpled the ball of foil and stuck it in her pocket. Wiping her hands on her jeans, she turned to Melanie. "That should keep him out of the way for a while."

Melanie watched anxiously as the dog gulped the meat. "What'd you put in it?" she asked.

Aynslee shrugged. "Oh, a little of this and a little of that. Mostly the stuff my stepmother uses when she can't sleep," Aynslee said carelessly.

"Aynslee!" Melanie said. She was shocked. What if the medicine made Tiger sick or even killed him? "How could you do that? What if you gave him too much?"

"I didn't," Aynslee said.

"Are you sure?" Melanie asked.

"It's just going to make him sleepy so that he won't mess with us," Aynslee promised. "Relax, will you?" She closed the door and headed across the ring toward the downstairs ramp.

Melanie gave a last doubtful look at the office door. Then she followed Aynslee down the ramp. But she was worried about the dog. And she was beginning to think that maybe her wonderful plan wasn't such a great idea after all.

The downstairs stables at Clarebrook always reminded Melanie of a medieval dungeon. The floor

17

was made of gray cobblestones, worn smooth from a hundred years of horses' hooves walking on them. At opposite ends of the barn were windows, but they were below street level, so not much light or air came in from outside. The ceilings were low and shrouded with cobwebs. Melanie usually avoided looking up because once she had seen a rat nearly the size of a half-grown cat scuttling along one of the crossbeams.

But as gloomy as the downstairs looked, it was still a horse stable, and the good, familiar smells of horse and hay and leather met Melanie as she reached the bottom of the ramp. Clarebrook was old and dark, but the horses' stalls were clean, their coats were shiny from good grooming, and when they weren't being ridden they were calmly munching the sweet-smelling hay.

"Who are you going to ride?" Melanie asked Aynslee.

"Ramses—who do you think?" Aynslee said, starting toward the horse's stall. "Go get your horse and meet me in the ring," she ordered Melanie.

Melanie started down the aisle. It was dim and quiet in the barn with all the grooms gone. "Go 'way, rats," she muttered, looking uneasily around her.

Upstairs the horses lived in box stalls, but downstairs they were in straight stalls just big enough for them to stand up or lie down. The stalls were arranged in three rows along three aisles. Melanie made her way to the second aisle without running into any rats and turned left. In the last stall was her favorite horse, Milky

Way. As soon as she saw him, a big smile broke over her face and she forgot to be worried anymore. "Hi, Milky," she said happily, unclipping the stall guard.

Milky Way was a tall chocolate-colored Appaloosa with a blanket of white splotches across his rump. He was sixteen years old and had lived at Clarebrook for more than half his life. He was a notorious kicker who would pin his ears and lunge at any horse that came near him when he was in the ring. Ten years of going around the tiny circle in the arena at Clarebrook had made him stiff and surly, but he was also fearless in the park and comfortable to ride. Most people were afraid of being around him on the ground. He had a habit of nipping at people as they tightened the girth. Melanie herself had been bitten a few times. Milky Way was temperamental and would sometimes squeal in protest when asked to canter. But perhaps because no one else really appreciated him, Melanie loved him with all her heart.

Melanie took a brush from a milk crate nailed to the wall outside his stall. "How are you, handsome boy?" she said as she approached him. Her first impulse was always to throw her arms around the horse and hug him like a big dog, but having done it once, she knew better. She had learned to approach him slowly. "Hi, Milky Way," she said, carefully stepping closer.

Milky Way eyed Melanie suspiciously. Then he put his ears back and moved as far to the side of his stall as he could. "Don't be like that," Melanie said gently.

"Come on. It's me, Melanie. You know me." She moved closer to the horse, her hand outstretched. Milky Way snapped his teeth in her direction and Melanie flinched but kept coming. At last she got her hand on him. "Good boy," she said. "What a smart boy you are." Melanie stroked the horse's neck, speaking softly to him, and after a moment his ears relaxed. "Milky, guess what?" Melanie said as she began brushing him. "As soon as school's out, I'm leasing you for the whole summer! In a couple of weeks, you're all mine." She laid her head against his neck and lovingly put her arms around him.

"I'm going to take you to the park every day," Melanie went on. "And make sure you get turned out every night. For a whole summer, you won't have to have any strangers riding you. Nobody will bounce on your back or tighten your girth too fast. I promise. And I'm going to ride you bareback in the ring. And I'll keep you so clean, you'll be the handsomest Appaloosa in the whole barn. Sorry I can't give you a real grooming today," she added. "But we're in a hurry."

She took the bridle down from its hook outside Milky Way's stall and slipped it over her shoulder. With some effort, she stood on tiptoe and managed to wrangle the saddle off its high rack without it falling on her head. Then she lugged it into the stall and set it on the horse's back. He kicked at the wall in annoyance, but Melanie ignored it. She fastened the girth loosely, keeping a wary eye on the horse in case he decided to bite.

He held his nose high in the air and refused to open his teeth, but Melanie was as stubborn as he was and soon she had the bridle on him.

"Mel, are you ready?" she heard Aynslee call.

"Yeah, coming," Melanie replied. She backed Milky Way out of the stall and led him toward the ramp.

Aynslee was at the bottom of the ramp with her own favorite horse. As Melanie approached her, she saw Aynslee mounting up on the tall, skinny chestnut named Ramses.

"Aynslee, what are you doing?" Melanie asked. No one was supposed to mount up in the stables. The ceilings were low and the walls close together. It could be dangerous.

Aynslee put her feet into the stirrups and gathered up the reins. "Something I've always wanted to do," she said. Then she kicked Ramses in the sides, ducked her head under the doorway, and rode up the ramp!

"You're crazy!" Melanie yelled. She stared after Aynslee in amazement as she listened to Ramses's feet scrambling on the wooden ramp.

When she was sure Aynslee was out of the way, Melanie took the reins and carefully led Milky Way up the ramp.

"Chicken," Aynslee observed when she saw that Melanie hadn't ridden up.

Melanie ignored her. She tightened the girth and tried to concentrate on how much fun it would be when they were finally riding through the park in the moonlight.

But she was having second thoughts. What if someone saw them and reported them? What if Aynslee did something else stupid and dangerous? She didn't like the way Aynslee was taking over, and she didn't like the way she'd ridden up the ramps with Ramses. And one more thought occurred to Melanie. If they got caught, there was no way her dad would let her lease Milky Way. The whole moonlight ride idea had seemed fun until right then. Now Melanie wasn't sure about it at all.

"Aynslee," Melanie whispered, "Let's not go."

"What's the matter?" Aynslee said coolly. "Losing your nerve?"

"No," Melanie said defensively. "I just think maybe this isn't such a great idea after all."

"Of course it's a great idea," Aynslee said. "And you came up with it, remember?"

"Aynslee . . . ," Melanie said. "What if we get caught? I won't get to lease Milky Way this summer."

"We're not going to get caught," Aynslee argued. "And if you try and back out now, I'll tell. I'll tell everyone it was all your idea," Aynslee said. "Get some guts, why don't you?"

Melanie stared at her. Aynslee was probably bluffing. But even if she didn't tell, if Melanie backed out Aynslee would be mad at her for weeks. It definitely wasn't worth backing out now. Without another word, Melanie mounted up and quickly adjusted her stirrups. She gave a last tug on her left stirrup and shortened her reins. "Let's go," she said.

On one of the steel poles in the middle of the ring was a button that controlled the big garage door. Aynslee hit it, and with a groan the door slid all the way open.

Nervously, Melanie followed Aynslee down the ramp and out the front entrance. The horses' feet rang out loudly as they stepped into the street, and Melanie's heart began to pound. Would the neighbors notice that the horses were going out so late in the evening? Would they call the police?

They had to follow the one-way traffic through the streets to get to the park. As they turned right onto Amsterdam Avenue, cars whizzed by them, but the horses just walked along as if nothing unusual were happening. Several people passed by. Melanie was afraid someone would say something, but no one did more than give the horses a passing glance.

A minute later the girls and their horses were turning right again on Ninetieth Street. From there it was a straight two blocks to Central Park. The sounds of the traffic on the busy avenue behind them faded as they headed down the quieter numbered street, and Melanie began to feel a little less worried. Now that they had made it out of the barn, the thrill of being on a horse in the middle of the city took over.

The day had been warm and the barn stuffy, but a cool breeze came from the river behind them as they headed for the park. Melanie noticed that Milky Way's ears were forward, and he walked along eagerly, as if he were glad to be going out. She couldn't help feeling glad with him.

"We're going to have such a great summer together, Milky Way," Melanie told the horse as they made their way up Ninetieth Street. She reached forward and patted his neck gently, thinking about how wonderful the summer was going to be. "I'm going to take you to the park every morning when it's still cool out," she promised him. "You'll never have to ride in the heat. And I'll give you a bath every afternoon so that you can go back to your stall all clean and cool."

They were about to cross Columbus Avenue when Aynslee suddenly yanked Ramses back. Milky Way almost bumped into the chestnut's hindquarters before Melanie could pull up. Exasperated, Melanie tried to maneuver Milky Way away from Ramses before he bit him. "What'd you do that for?" she asked.

Aynslee didn't answer. Instead she began backing Ramses up. The chestnut's hindquarters bumped right into Milky Way, who squealed an angry warning. "Aynslee!" Melanie exclaimed, pulling Milky Way's head aside just in time to keep him from taking a chunk out of Ramses with his teeth. "Cut it out!"

But Aynslee, still backing Ramses, was pointing urgently down the avenue. Suddenly Melanie understood why she had stopped. "Oh no," she said. "It's Red!"

3

"BACK UP!" AYNSLEE HISSED, HAULING BACK ON RAMSES'S reins. Red was crossing Columbus Avenue a block down on Eighty-Ninth Street, pushing his wheelbarrow back toward the barn. If they had walked into the intersection right then, he would have been sure to see them.

Melanie leaned back, closed her legs against Milky Way's sides, and held back the reins so that he would back up. But she had forgotten that Milky Way didn't like backing. He swished his tail in annoyance, pinned his ears, and stepped forward a few steps into the intersection.

"Melanie! He's going to see you!" Aynslee warned. "Get back here until he crosses!"

"I can't help it," Melanie whispered frantically, pulling back on the reins. But try as she might, Melanie couldn't get Milky Way to back up. He ground his teeth

25

together and stuck his head as high in the air as he could, stubbornly refusing. Melanie gave up. She quickly turned him around, then gave him a big thump with her legs to make him trot back onto Ninetieth Street.

"Did he see us?" Melanie asked anxiously.

Aynslee made Ramses walk forward a step or two, then peered cautiously around the corner. Red had just about crossed the intersection and was heading down Eighty-Ninth Street toward Clarebrook.

"I don't think he saw us. Whew!" Aynslee said, looking back at Melanie with a relieved grin. "That was close!" They waited until Red was out of sight and the light had changed to yellow. Then they trotted across the avenue just in time.

After that it was a quiet five-minute walk to the park. Melanie kept expecting someone to question them for being out of the barn so close to dark, but nobody seemed to notice. Soon the ring of the horses' shoes on the pavement gave way to the soft scraping of their hooves in the sandy footing of the bridle path.

"We made it," Melanie said, feeling relieved and nervous at the same time.

Aynslee turned and gave her a skeptical look. "Did you really think we wouldn't?" she asked.

"I was a little worried for a minute there," Melanie confessed.

Aynslee stuck out her hand, palm up, and Melanie grinned and slapped it. "Let's ride," Aynslee said. She put Ramses into a trot and Melanie followed on Milky Way.

The part of the bridle path they were on circled the reservoir in the middle of Central Park. Melanie looked at the view across the water as they trotted along. A bit of breeze barely tickled the surface. The last rays from the setting sun behind her turned the buildings on the far side of the reservoir rosy red. Already she could see a wedge of the orange-gold moon rising above the buildings.

"Look at the moon, Aynslee," Melanie said, pointing across the water.

"That's what we came for," Aynslee said.

A quarter of the way around the reservoir, they turned off onto another path that circled a wide grassy area of soccer and baseball fields known as the North Meadow. The light was fading rapidly as they trotted along, and already most of the moon had appeared above the buildings on the East Side. The horses hung close together, ears forward, and stepped along, alert but calm. High on Milky Way's sturdy back, Melanie felt safe. She was sure that nothing bad could happen. But then she saw it.

"Aynslee, stop," Melanie called out.

"Why?" Aynslee asked.

Melanie pointed. Up ahead was a bend in the path where a little three-wheeled police vehicle sat. Melanie had seen it there plenty of times during the day, but she hadn't counted on it being there at night. They would have to turn back or find another way to avoid it.

"This way," Melanie said. She turned Milky Way off the bridle path and rode through a gap in the bushes.

"Where're we going?" Aynslee asked.

"Just follow me," Melanie said mysteriously. She guided Milky Way onto a very narrow path that led through some trees and up a steep hill. She had galloped up the hill many times before with Jonathan, her instructor. As Melanie started up the path she leaned forward, wrapping her fingers around a section of Milky Way's mane. Then she gave him an energetic thump with her legs.

Milky Way dug in his hindquarters and took off, surging up the hill at a fast canter. Melanie bent close to the horse's plunging neck, loving the feeling of speed and power underneath her. The first time Jonathan had taken her up the hill she had been a little afraid, but once she got used to the motion she thought it was thrilling. The horse was going fast and hard, but the hill kept him from getting out of control or putting his head down where he could buck. All Melanie had to do was keep bending forward in jumping position and hang onto the horse's mane.

Too soon she reached the top of the hill. She sat back and brought Milky Way down to a walk. Then she gave him a huge pat on the shoulder. "You are awesome!" she declared. Milky Way merely snorted and began to nibble at the grass.

Then Aynslee burst out of the trees and into the clearing at the top of the hill. "Man!" Aynslee said, panting as she pulled Ramses up. "Warn me next time you're going to gallop. I almost fell off!"

Melanie regarded her coolly. Aynslee was a big talker, but she wasn't much of a rider. It annoyed Melanie that Aynslee was so unforgiving of other people's weaknesses but expected everyone to take care of her. At the moment, Melanie was in no mood to indulge her. "Get some guts, why don't you?" she retorted in the exact same tone Aynslee had used with her back at the barn.

Aynslee scowled. "What'd you come up here for, anyway?" she asked.

Melanie walked Milky Way forward all the way to the highest point of the hill. "This," she said simply, gesturing with her arm to include the whole view of the park and the city that spread before them. "Come see."

Aynslee walked Ramses up after her, and the two girls sat on horseback, looking all around them. The sun had dropped below the horizon to the west, leaving the sky a soft hazy blue. Before them was the green expanse of the North Meadow, with the rest of the park spreading south beyond it. The lights were twinkling on in the buildings, and in the east the moon had risen above the tallest skyscrapers. It hung in the sky like a soft ripe peach, growing higher and lighter by the moment. "Isn't it beautiful?" Melanie said.

"Awesome," Aynslee admitted.

"Isn't this weird?" Melanie asked. "I mean, we live in this huge city, but we're sitting on horses on the top of a hill, surrounded by trees and woods. I feel like it could be a hundred years ago. We could be the Indians who lived here once."

They stood silently while the moon climbed higher and grew smaller and whiter. Then when it was good and dark, Aynslee said, "Come on, Pocahontas," and moved Ramses at a walk down the hill.

Melanie nudged Milky Way's sides with her legs and he ambled down after Ramses. Soon they had reached the bottom of the hill. Aynslee sauntered into the middle of the North Meadow and halted. Melanie pulled up beside her and looked around.

They were at the bottom of a bowl of cool night air, surrounded by a rim of dark trees. Past the trees Melanie glimpsed the gray ribbon of sand that marked the bridle path, and beyond that the tall blocks of the buildings on the avenues, lit with squares of yellow light. The sounds of the traffic drifted to her, muted by the trees, but in the middle of the North Meadow it was quiet enough to hear the breeze rustling the branches.

"Let's canter," Melanie said suddenly, gathering up her reins.

"Come on," Aynslee said.

The two girls took off across the moonlit meadow. Melanie heard Milky Way's feet thudding through the grass and felt the cool air rushing past her. It was strange and a little scary to be going so fast when she could barely see. She found herself relying on her balance and pure instinct instead of her eyes, and it seemed dangerous and thrilling. A broad grin spread across her face. This was what she had come for, and now that she was actually galloping through the park under the light of the moon, it was even better than she had imagined it would be.

Too soon they reached the edge of a baseball field and had to slow down. "That was so cool!" Melanie said, sliding her hand up Milky Way's neck to pat him.

"Let's canter around the bases," Aynslee suggested. The backstop fence loomed silver behind her. Aynslee trotted Ramses toward home plate and faced first.

"Go!" Melanie shouted.

Aynslee kicked Ramses and headed in the direction of first base. Then she rounded second and third. She dashed toward home plate and halted, Ramses's feet sending up a spray of dust as he slid to a stop.

"Nice slide," Melanie said appreciatively.

"Now you do it," Aynslee said.

Both girls were laughing as Melanie positioned Milky Way behind home plate.

"Go!" Aynslee shrieked, and Melanie took off, repeating Aynslee's gallop around the infield.

"That was fun," Melanie gasped as she reached home plate and pulled up.

"Let's do it again, "Aynslee said, bumping Ramses into Milky Way's butt.

"Hey, cut it out," Melanie said indignantly.

Aynslee began to giggle. "Move over," she ordered,

walking Ramses into Milky Way again. Milky Way squealed and Melanie burst out laughing.

"Want to play bumper horses?" Aynslee asked. She started to turn Ramses around and ride him into Milky Way again.

"Aynslee!" Melanie said, nearly collapsing with laughter. "He's going to bite Ramses."

Suddenly a bright light was shining right in Melanie's eyes. She stopped laughing and turned her head from side to side, squinting as she tried to see where the light was coming from. Next to her Aynslee was shading her own eyes with her forearm. The horses snorted. Ramses pranced nervously in place and Milky Way stomped the ground with a forefoot.

"Stop right there," came a voice over a megaphone.

"It's the cops!" Aynslee hissed.

Melanie froze. She had thought that the police vehicle they had avoided was the only one. What were these guys doing in the middle of the North Meadow?

"Come on, Mel. We're outta here." Aynslee turned Ramses away from the light and sent him into a gallop toward the west side of the park. Melanie didn't know what to do. Should they run away? Or would that only get them into worse trouble? She was still trying to decide when Milky Way made up her mind for her. He had had enough of the flashlight in his eyes and the mysterious rumbling of the police vehicle engine. He took off after Aynslee and Ramses at a dead gallop.

Melanie let him run. She couldn't have stopped him,

anyway. His long strides ate up the distance between him and Ramses, and soon Melanie was right behind Aynslee. She glanced back over her shoulder and saw the three-wheeled police vehicle with lights flashing on the top in hot pursuit, bouncing crazily on the bumpy ground.

"Stop the horses now," the officer ordered over the megaphone.

"Aynslee, what should we do?" Melanie shouted.

"Shut up and ride," Aynslee ordered. "He's not going to catch us."

They thundered across the North Meadow. Melanie was terrified that one of the horses would step in a hole and trip, but somehow they didn't. In less than a minute they had reached the bridle path on the west side of the park again. Aynslee turned onto it and they galloped up the path toward the reservoir.

"Is he still back there?" Aynslee asked.

Melanie glanced over her shoulder once more, but this time the little police vehicle was nowhere to be seen. "No," she told Aynslee. "I think we lost him."

"Whoo!" Aynslee crowed, slowing Ramses to a walk. She stuck out a hand for Melanie to smack.

Melanie slapped Aynslee's palm, laughing with relief and exhilaration at their narrow escape. "That was close," she said when she finally caught her breath.

"Why'd you wait so long to follow me?" Aynslee asked her. "I thought for a minute you were going to let them take you in."

"I was just trying to make the chase more interesting," Melanie said airily.

They rambled toward the park exit, the horses panting from the run. Before they left the bridle path, Melanie turned back for one last view of the moon. It hung white and perfect in the sky, and its wavering image sparkled in the reservoir. Melanie knew she would remember this night for the rest of her life.

"That was great!" Aynslee exclaimed as they stepped onto the street and began walking down Central Park West toward Eighty-Ninth Street. "I knew that cop would never keep up with us in that cheesy little three-wheeler," she said smugly as the horses' metal shoes clopped on the asphalt and cars zoomed past them.

"I bet he's still bouncing around the North Meadow looking for us," Melanie said with a laugh.

Aynslee cupped one hand around her mouth. "Come out with your hands up," she said, imitating the policeman in a megaphone voice.

"You mean, 'Come out with your hooves up!'" Melanie giggled.

Aynslee laughed, too, and Melanie forgot the tension she'd felt earlier. Although they'd had some scary moments, Melanie was exhilarated. The plan had worked. They had successfully sneaked two horses out and gone for a moonlight gallop in Central Park. They'd be talking about it for weeks.

The girls were just about to turn off Central Park

West onto Eighty-Ninth Street. Melanie heard the sound of the horses' feet change, from the familiar sound of metal shoes on the street to the sound of metal sliding on metal. The animals had stepped onto a huge steel plate covering a hole where construction workers had been digging up the street.

Ramses began to slip and slide like an ice-skater struggling for balance on the slick surface. Melanie heard Aynslee cry out and at the same time felt Milky Way spook, then lose his own footing as he tried to run on the slippery metal plate. Melanie leaned forward and clutched the reins. She froze in terror while she waited for the horses to fall. Then Ramses somehow made it off the metal plate and onto the safer footing of the asphalt. Melanie had just enough time to see Aynslee pull up and turn around, and to realize that she wasn't going to be that lucky. It was almost a relief when Milky Way let out a squeal of fright as his feet went out from under him at last and he fell hard on the street.

Melanie was thrown from the saddle and sent skidding to the side of the road. She noted the scraping of her arm across the rough street and wondered when it would begin to hurt. Milky Way was floundering on his belly, terrified, still trying to get his feet under him. For a second Melanie saw him almost stand up. His front feet found traction on the street and he gave a heave, struggling to get his hind legs underneath him.

Melanie saw how frightened and confused the horse

was. If she could get to him, she might be able to lead him off the metal plate and calm him down. She tried to get up, but she couldn't seem to move.

"Don't worry, Milky Way," she called to the horse, hoping her voice would reassure him. "I'm going to help you." She stared at her arm, puzzled that no matter how she concentrated on moving it, it refused to obey her. She rolled forward awkwardly and felt a wave of hot pain shoot through her shoulder and arm.

She gasped. For a second all she could see was black dotted with sparks of light. Then as the pain slowly subsided, her vision cleared and she saw Milky Way finally scramble to his feet. She knew she had to get up and catch him before he took off for Clarebrook. She tried once more to move, pushing herself up slowly with her good arm. "Whoa, Milky Way," she called to him. Where was Aynslee? She looked around and saw her sitting nearby on Ramses.

"Aynslee, can you get off and catch him?" Melanie called. "I can't get up. I think I broke my arm."

Aynslee didn't answer. She was staring past Milky Way, a shocked expression on her face. Melanie wondered what she could be looking at. "Aynslee," she called again. "Catch him, please?"

"Mel!" Aynslee finally screamed. That was when the taxi cab came speeding around the corner.

"MEL?"

Melanie felt her father's weight beside her as he sat down on the edge of her bed. She was awake, though she didn't want to be. It was late—after midnight—and Melanie was numb with exhaustion but unable to sleep. Her right shoulder throbbed with pain and a constant parade of tears leaked from her eyes.

"Melanie?" her Dad said again.

Melanie felt him take her left hand and squeeze it firmly. Slowly she opened her eyes. The first thing she noticed was how tired and sad her dad looked. And that started up another stream of tears. She had never meant for the accident with Milky Way to happen. But it had. The worst possible thing had happened, and Melanie felt awful.

Will Graham wore small silver wire-rimmed glasses.

He took them off and rubbed his eyes with the thumb and fingers of the other hand, the hand that wasn't holding Melanie's. "How's your shoulder?" he asked gently.

Melanie stared mutely at her dad. Her right shoulder had been dislocated in the accident and her right arm had been scraped badly on the concrete. She couldn't bring herself to answer right then, but what she was thinking was that she would have put up with a thousand times the pain in her body compared to the pain of losing Milky Way.

"Mel, I just don't know what to do anymore," her dad said. "What can we do to get you to stay out of trouble? I think maybe this city is just too full of sadness for us right now. I can't get away from it, but you can."

Get away? What was he talking about? Melanie felt her heart turn to ice as he went on.

"I'm sending you to stay with your Uncle Mike and Aunt Ashleigh in Kentucky for the summer. I'll be in Europe for a few weeks, as you know. At the end of August we'll see how it's going and make a decision on whether you should come back to New York," her dad said.

Melanie's voice came back then. "Dad, no!" she protested, feeling panicked. Was he crazy? She knew that taking the horses to the park had been a mistake. But how could he send her to Kentucky? Hadn't she been punished enough?

"Dad, please! Don't make me go there. I know that Aynslee and I shouldn't have taken the horses out, but that was such a freak accident—if that cab hadn't come around the corner . . ." Melanie's voice broke again as she thought of Milky Way lying on the street. "Why are you sending me away?" she sobbed. "Please don't send me away."

"Melanie, it's not just the accident and the horses." Her father sighed deeply and looked at her. "It's—it's everything. You don't seem happy here. You've never liked the girls at your school, living with nannies. There's so much that could be better." He reached out and gently wiped at her tears with his thumb.

Deep down Melanie knew he was right. She'd never truly been happy. At least not since she was little—not since before her mother died. But she wasn't ready to believe that she would be better off anywhere else. The idea of leaving her father and what was left of her life filled her with panic. "Dad, that's not true!" she lied. "Of course I'm happy. I'm fine. I'm perfectly fine," she insisted.

"Mel, you're not fine," her dad said quietly. "You're just going downhill here in New York. I thought it was just that you were bored in school, but after what happened tonight—"

"Dad, I'm sorry!" Melanie wailed. "I'm sorry! Please don't send me away!"

"I'm not around here enough for you," he went on. "But even if I were, I don't think it would help."

"Dad, that's not true! You are around enough. Really," Melanie said.

He shook his head. "You deserve so much more, Mel," he told her, and he looked so, so sad.

Melanie knew that look and that tone. She knew he was thinking about her mother.

"I think a change of environment would be good for you." Her dad looked out the window at the cityscape of dark buildings lit by twinkling lights. Then he went on. "It's no wonder you keep getting into trouble. New York is such a difficult town to grow up in—I really think you'll be better off in Kentucky. And Uncle Mike and Aunt Ashleigh live on a Thoroughbred training farm," he added in a cheerful voice. "You'll get to be around horses all the time. I bet you'll really like it once you get used to it."

For her father it was that simple. She needed a change from New York. Going to Kentucky for the summer was the answer. It would keep her out of trouble, even if it meant sending her to live with relatives she barely knew.

For Melanie it was another story. She didn't want to go to Kentucky. She wanted to stay in New York, where things were normal, familiar, although she was pretty sure that after the accident with Milky Way nothing was going to feel quite normal ever again.

Two weeks later, on the plane to Louisville, Melanie stared out the window at the cloud formations. She had stopped crying about the accident, but she hadn't stopped wishing that she could go back to that horrible night and stop herself and Aynslee from taking the horses out. It had seemed like a harmless, fun thing to do at the time. But now it seemed horribly stupid. And now Milky Way was gone.

She closed her eyes. The terrible vision of the struggling horse lit by the cab's headlights still haunted her. Over and over Melanie's mind went back to that evening, her arm throbbing mercilessly as she tried to get to her feet. She had finally managed to stand up, but by then it was too late.

It seemed to Melanie that Milky Way somehow knew what was about to happen. The horse gave a last desperate lunge toward her, his wild eyes begging her to help him. Why couldn't she help him? was the mute question in his panicked face. Melanie put out her hand as if she could somehow shield the horse with it. But of course she couldn't.

"Nooo!" Melanie had screamed in anguish, as the cab continued its deadly rush toward them. Its headlights blazed around the dark shape of the horse and Melanie's outstretched hand. There were two more screams: One was from the cab's tires as the driver saw the horse in his path and hit the brakes. The other was from the horse as the car slammed into him.

"Miss? Fasten your seat belt please. We're getting ready to land." The nasal voice of the flight attendant dissolved the vision of the accident from Melanie's mind. But it could not dissolve the pain in her heart.

That was worse, far worse, than the pain in her dislocated shoulder and her badly scraped arm.

"Okay," Melanie told the flight attendant. Her right arm was still in a sling and she fumbled awkwardly with the seat belt. The woman in the seat next to her finally reached over and helped her fasten it.

"Thanks," Melanie managed to say. The woman nodded and went back to reading her novel.

Melanie pressed her face against the window and watched the runway growing larger as they made their descent into Louisville. Suddenly she missed her father terribly. Then, because that was too hard to keep feeling, she let her anger at her father swell up, huge and black. How could he have just sent her away like that? Melanie had tried every way she could think of to persuade her dad to let her stay in New York. She had even begged him to take her to Europe with him. But he was resolute. Then he'd announced that Susan was going to Europe with him. That had pretty much convinced Melanie that her dad was just glad he was getting rid of his troublesome daughter for the summer.

And then there was Aynslee. Aynslee's horse hadn't been hurt at all. She had also told everyone that going to the park that night had been Melanie's idea. It had, but Melanie thought Aynslee should have taken some of the blame. She would have done that for Aynslee. *Some friend*, Melanie thought. Worse, she realized that she was going to miss Aynslee, anyway. Melanie wondered if it was possible to feel any more miserable.

She was still looking out the window, her chin cupped in her good hand, as the plane bumped to a stop at the gate. She continued to stare stubbornly out the window until she was the last passenger left on the plane. She was half hoping that maybe if she just sat there, the plane would take off again with her on it and bring her back to New York. But the flight attendant came by and noticed her.

"You can deplane now, miss," the blond woman told her curtly.

Melanie scowled and grudgingly undid her seat belt. She carefully hung her backpack over her good shoulder. Then she got to her feet, stiffly after sitting for two hours, and headed slowly down the aisle toward the exit.

As she came out of the tunnel into the airport terminal, Melanie armed herself with her most unreadable expression and scanned the faces of the few people standing around the gate area. She didn't see her aunt and uncle, or her cousin. She looked around again, more carefully, and still didn't see them.

"Great," Melanie muttered. "They can't even make it to the airport on time." She hitched her backpack up higher on her shoulder and started down the corridor toward the baggage claim.

She was almost there when she heard someone calling, "Melanie!" She turned around and recognized her tall blond-haired uncle, Mike Reese, waving at her. He strode quickly toward her and hugged her gingerly,

43

careful not to squeeze her shoulder. Melanie didn't hug him back. "Sorry I was late," he said. "We hit some traffic on the highway. There was an accide—" he started to say. Then he stopped abruptly.

Melanie knew what he was thinking. She was sure her dad had told her aunt and uncle all about the accident with Milky Way. She gazed coolly into her uncle's friendly blue eyes, waiting for him to finish. When he didn't speak, she said, "We?"

Uncle Mike nodded. "Christina came with me. She went to wait at the baggage claim in case I didn't find you at the gate. But here you are," he said smiling.

"Here I am," she said, mimicking his tone. *What a goof,* Melanie thought.

"Well, let's head over to the baggage claim. Christina will be so glad to see you."

Her backpack slipped down her arm and Mike grabbed it. "Let me take that for you," he said. Melanie let him take it and followed him down the corridor.

At the baggage claim she spotted her cousin, Christina Reese. Melanie looked at Christina's strawberry blond hair and remembered with regret that her own hair for once was just plain blond. She hadn't been able to streak it with Kool-Aid since she hurt her shoulder. She wished she had found some way to dye it, anyway. She was sorry to have missed out on the obvious shock value of having bright green hair in the Louisville Airport. And clearly it would have embarrassed her cousin.

Christina was at least half a head taller than her cousin, though she was a few months younger. "Hi, Melanie," Christina said, stepping toward her with a small smile.

Melanie didn't want Christina to hug her, so she folded her good arm across her front. "Hey, Mouse," Melanie said to her cousin in a sugary sweet voice. "Long time, no see." Melanie was pleased at the tiny look of annoyance that crossed Christina's face at the nickname. It was short for "Country Mouse." Melanie had started calling her cousin that when the Reeses had visited New York back in the spring.

"Um, how was your flight?" Christina asked politely.

"Fine," Melanie replied. She turned to her uncle and pointed at a black suitcase with several bright-colored ribbons tied on the handle. "That's mine," she said to him.

Melanie knew she was being rude, but she didn't care. She wanted to make it perfectly clear that coming to Kentucky hadn't been her idea and that she wasn't going to enjoy any of it.

"This way," Uncle Mike said, ignoring Melanie's tone. "Christina, take this for your cousin, please," he said, handing her Melanie's backpack.

"Sure," Christina said. The two girls fell in behind Mike. "So when do you get to take the sling off your arm?" Christina asked Melanie as they headed out of the airport.

"In a couple of weeks, I guess," Melanie said.

45

"Does it hurt much?" Christina asked.

"Yes," Melanie replied. *What's the matter with her,* Melanie thought. Was this girl just going to keep asking her dumb questions? Didn't she have sense enough to know that the accident with Milky Way wasn't something that Melanie would want to discuss? Maybe if she told Christina a few gory details, she would shut up.

"It's excruciating, actually," she went on. "Have you ever had the pleasure of feeling your shoulder jerked right out of the socket as you slide along the street getting the skin ripped off your arm?"

Christina shook her head, shuddering. "No. But once I had stitches in my head. I fell off my pony and landed on a sharp rock. Right here, see?" She pointed to a spot over her eyebrow.

Melanie looked with disbelief at the nearly invisible scar. "Oh yeah. I can only imagine how awful that must have been," she said mockingly.

"Oh, it wasn't too bad," Christina said, completely missing the sarcasm. "It really only hurt right when it happened."

Melanie rolled her eyes toward the ceiling. *This was going to be great, just great,* she thought grimly—stuck in Kentucky for the whole summer with her hick cousin. "Where's your mom?" she asked to change the subject.

"Oh, she's at Monmouth with a few of the horses," Christina said. "She'll be back at the end of the week."

"What's Monmouth?" Melanie asked.

"A racetrack," Christina said, as if it were hard to believe that someone wouldn't know that. "It's in New Jersey," she added.

Good, Melanie was thinking. One less relative to deal with, at least for a few days.

"Here we are," Uncle Mike said, setting her suitcase into the back of a silver pickup truck. "Climb in, ladies."

Melanie stared at the truck. Did they expect her to sit in the back? But then Uncle Mike unlocked the passenger door and Christina climbed in and slid into the middle of the front seat.

"Need a hand getting in there, Mel?" Uncle Mike offered her his arm.

"No, I'm fine," Melanie said, pulling herself up with her left arm. She sat down next to Christina and Uncle Mike closed the door. Then he went around and got in the driver's side. Melanie inched over toward the door as far as she could, wishing she could disappear. Why couldn't they drive a car like normal people? She had been hoping to avoid talking to them by sitting in the backseat.

Fortunately, though, nobody said much on the drive back. Melanie kept her eyes out the window, watching the highway unwind behind them. Soon they were out of the city area and traveling through sprawling green pastures. They passed farm after farm. Melanie was a little amazed at how many horses she saw. Soon she felt the truck slow down and they turned up a long driveway. A small signpost at the entrance read "Whitebrook Farm" in elegant lettering.

"This is it," Uncle Mike said to Melanie. "Welcome to Whitebrook Farm."

They drove slowly past white-fenced paddocks where horses were turned out. In one of them was a group of ten or twelve colts and fillies. They froze when they saw the truck drive by, then whirled and ran with baby strides down to the end of the paddock, their fluffy tails swishing with excitement.

"Oh," Melanie gasped before she could stop herself. She had never seen baby horses in person. They were adorable.

Christina gave her an amused sidelong glance. "Those are the babies," she reported. "Aren't they cute?"

"They're gorgeous," Melanie admitted, craning her head back to get one last glimpse of them. "Where do you get them?"

Christina and her dad exchanged amused glances. "We breed them right here at Whitebrook," Christina said.

"That's our best crop of foals in five years," Uncle Mike said. "There's at least one Triple Crown winner in that lot, if you ask me."

"Dad, you say that every year," Christina commented.

"Do I?" Mike asked. "Well, it must be true every year then." He stopped the truck and shifted into park. "End of the line," he reported.

Melanie opened the truck door with her left arm and stepped out onto the gravel drive. The Reeses lived in a big white two-story wooden farmhouse with red shutters that matched the red of the barns and outbuildings. Melanie wondered if she was going to have her own bedroom or if she would have to share with Mouse.

"Come on. I'll show you to your room," Christina said. Melanie was relieved. At least if she had her own room it would be easier to hole up until the end of the summer. That was her plan—to stay away from people as much as possible and just wait for the summer to be over so that she could go back to New York. Melanie followed Christina up the stairs and down the hall. Christina pushed open a door. "This'll be your room," she volunteered. "Mine's down the hall on the left.

Melanie peered cautiously inside. There were two large windows hung with white lace curtains through which she glimpsed a view of a pasture. There was a dainty highboy dresser and a small desk with a chair. The bed was an old-fashioned iron bed painted white and spread with a yellow-flowered comforter. Melanie walked in and sat down on it.

"Um, where shall I put this?" Christina asked, holding out the backpack.

Melanie shrugged and winced as her shoulder moved. "Anywhere," she muttered.

Uncle Mike brought her suitcase in and set it down at the foot of the bed. "If you need help with unpacking or anything, just let us know," he said.

Melanie nodded politely, wishing they would leave her alone.

"I've got to go down to the barn office and take care of some paperwork," Uncle Mike continued. "Christina can show you around the house and grounds whenever you feel like you're ready. Right, Chris?"

"Sure, Dad," Christina acknowledged.

Melanie thought he was about to leave when suddenly he turned and put a hand on her cheek. "I want you to feel at home here, Melanie," Uncle Mike told her earnestly. "I know you've had a tough time lately and you must be feeling pretty low. Your Aunt Ashleigh and I are glad you came, and we both want you to relax and enjoy yourself. There's nothing like life on a farm," he said, smiling. "In no time you'll feel like a million bucks." He stood up, ruffled her hair like she was a little kid, and left the room.

Melanie impatiently smoothed her hair where she imagined he had mussed it. Then she got up and went to look out the window. "New York is my home," she muttered, looking out at the strange landscape of trees and green grass.

"What?" Christina asked.

"Nothing," Melanie said.

"Um, would you like me to show you around?" Christina offered.

Melanie kept staring out the window with her back to Christina. She had never felt more lonely in her life. "I would like you to leave me alone," she said quietly.

She stood at the window, waiting, until she heard Christina's footsteps going down the stairs. Then she walked to the bed and lay down on top of the flowered comforter. Soon the tears began to seep out of the corners of her eyes and run down her temples in a steady stream.

Her favorite horse was gone forever. And she had been responsible for his death. Melanie felt that something inside her had died along with him. She didn't think she could ever love another horse. More than that, she promised herself that she would never ride another horse again as long as she lived. "I owe you that much, Milky Way," she whispered.

Christina came up a while later and tapped tentatively on the open door. "Dinner's ready," she told Melanie.

"I'm not hungry," Melanie said, hoping Christina wouldn't see that she was crying. When she was sure Christina was downstairs again, Melanie got up and quietly closed the door. Then she lay on her back and let the tears come again, until the evening light faded into darkness.

5

SHE HADN'T THOUGHT SHE WAS TIRED, BUT THE NEXT THING Melanie knew she was opening her eyes to the soft golden sunshine streaming through the lace curtains. At first she was confused. She sat up, and the pain in her shoulder quickly reminded her where she was and why she was there.

She eased herself off the bed and dug into her suitcase for a pair of denim shorts and a black T-shirt. She found the bathroom down the hall and quickly washed her face and brushed her teeth. Then she headed down the stairs.

She found the kitchen. It looked just as an old farmhouse kitchen should look, with a big wooden table and four creaky, comfortable ladder-back chairs. A faint but delicious baking smell hung in the air. It reminded Melanie that although she hadn't been hungry the night before, now she was starving. No one seemed to be around, but she spotted a note on the table next to a covered basket.

She read the note. "Melanie—muffins in the basket, juice in fridge. Make yourself at home. We're at the barn. Come on down when you're ready." It was signed by her uncle.

Melanie lifted the napkin covering the muffins and took one out. She bit into it—blueberry—and chewed thoughtfully. It was delicious. She devoured three, then poured herself a glass of juice and gulped it.

She had just put the juice away when a photograph caught her eye. It was stuck on the door of the refrigerator in a magnetic frame—a picture of Christina with a dark gray mare, and a dark-haired hazel-eyed woman Melanie recognized as her aunt, Ashleigh Griffen. Christina and the horse both seemed to be posing for the camera. The horse's ears were perked forward and Christina wore a happy smile. Ashleigh's eyes weren't on the camera but on her daughter, and it was the expression on her face that caught Melanie's attention. Ashleigh's eyes were full of admiration and her smile was full of love. Melanie stared at the picture and felt it stir something in her—sadness, and something else— jealousy? Suddenly Melanie missed her own mother keenly.

"What's up?" a voice said.

Melanie jumped. Then she winced, rubbing her shoulder gently, and turned to see who had spoken. A boy about her age with curly auburn hair and freckles stood in the kitchen. He was wearing chaps over his jeans and carrying a safety helmet by its harness.

"Who're you?" Melanie asked.

"You're Melanie, right?" the boy asked. When she didn't answer, he went on. "Mike sent me up here to check on you. Christina and I are going for a ride. Want to come? By the way, I'm Kevin McLean," he offered.

"Do you live here, or what?" Melanie asked, ignoring his question.

"What," Kevin said. "My dad's the head trainer at Whitebrook. We live over there." He pointed vaguely out the kitchen window, where Melanie could see a two-story stone cottage.

"Do you always just walk in like that without knocking or anything?" Melanie demanded.

"Yep," Kevin said. "So, do you want to come?"

"I can't," Melanie said. When he gave her a skeptical look, she added, "I can't use this arm much yet."

Kevin nodded. "Mike told me you hurt your shoulder. But you can ride old Moonlight. She knows how to neck rein, so you can just use your left arm. She's really gentle. She was my first horse," Kevin told her.

Melanie was interested. But she remembered her silent promise to Milky Way never to ride another horse. She shook her head. "No thanks."

"Suit yourself," Kevin said with a shrug. He turned and pushed open the screen door, letting it bang shut behind him. Then he called to her from the yard: "Want to come down to the barn, anyway?"

Melanie hesitated. She didn't want to seem too interested. If she stayed unhappy, maybe they'd send her home sooner. But she did want to get another look at the baby horses she'd seen in the paddock on the way up. Maybe Kevin would show her where they were. "I guess so," Melanie said.

"Come on, then," Kevin called.

Melanie pushed open the screen door and stepped out into the brilliant summer sunshine.

"This way," Kevin said, heading toward a gate in the white picket-fenced yard.

Melanie followed him out of the yard, down a path, and then uphill again toward a group of three barns.

"That's the training track over there," Kevin said, pointing to a fenced-in dirt oval below the barns.

Melanie saw a tall man with wavy auburn hair leading a huge, shiny jet-black colt. He was trying to get the horse to walk through the starting gate, which was open at both ends.

"What're they doing to that horse?" Melanie asked.

"That's one of the young horses getting taught how to load into the gate," Kevin explained to Melanie. "Hi, Dad," he called with a wave to the man.

The man acknowledged Kevin with a quick smile and a nod but was too busy handling the horse to wave or answer. The jockey crouched over the horse's back as it pranced warily, sidestepping and snorting. Suddenly the colt stopped and swung its hindquarters sideways. Mr. McLean expertly circled the horse and led it forward again. This time he was able to coax it into the gate, but before he got it to walk all the way through, the horse reared, jerking the lead rope out of Mr. McLean's hand.

Melanie gasped as the big horse stood on its hindquarters. The jockey shouted something at Mr. McLean, who was trying to grab the loose end of the lead rope. But before he could, the horse put his front feet on the ground again and wheeled away. When he spun, the jockey lost her balance and fell off. The horse was headed toward the gap that led out of the training oval. He bolted through it and headed up the path, straight toward Kevin and Melanie.

"Uh-oh," Kevin said, backing off the path. "Pirate's loose again."

The horse thundered toward them. Melanie stood rooted to the spot.

"Melanie, move," Kevin urged her. "He'll knock you flat."

But Melanie didn't move. She couldn't move. Fixed in her mind was the image of Milky Way's struggling silhouette in the cab's headlights just before he was hit. Melanie stared at the runaway horse, wondering what it was going to feel like when he ran into her. Maybe it would knock her out. Then she could stop thinking about all the bad things that had happened to her. For a moment she wondered if Milky Way had felt the same way before the cab hit him.

"He's going to run over you," Kevin warned. He grabbed Melanie's good arm and tugged, trying to get her to move off the path.

The horse's shiny black face with the white star loomed closer and closer. Melanie saw his nostrils flaring as he breathed, and noticed a distracted look in his huge brown eyes.

"Stop," Melanie whispered, her eyes riveted on the horse's face. He wasn't looking at her, but everywhere and nowhere, as if he were lost. "Stop," she commanded, louder this time. She felt her heart begin to pound. Would he stop? Suddenly, common sense took over and told Melanie to jump out of the way, but something deeper in her overpowered it. She stayed put. The horse thundered right up to where Melanie was standing. Then, one stride away from running over her, he planted his haunches and stopped dead, spraying Melanie's feet with a shower of dirt.

"Wow," Kevin said.

Melanie realized she had been holding her breath all that time. She let it out in a slow and shaky sigh. The horse put his head down and stepped cautiously closer to Melanie. She stood still and let him come. He snorted several loud investigative snorts, moving his nose from Melanie's legs to her waist to her head. Melanie almost giggled but managed to contain herself as the horse blew enormous warm breaths into her ear. Finally, he seemed satisfied. He lipped a strand of her hair idly and gazed peacefully around, waiting for whatever was going to happen next. A tiny smile played at Melanie's lips as she deftly picked up the end of the lead rope that trailed on the ground. Then she reached up and stroked the horse's muscular neck.

Kevin's father, Ian McLean, came hurrying up the path. When he saw that Melanie had caught the horse, he stopped for a moment, resting his hands on his knees while he caught his breath. Then he walked calmly toward the children.

"Are you kids all right?" Mr. McLean asked. He was still breathing hard.

"Sure, Dad," Kevin said.

"I thought you were going to get run over, young lady," Mr. McLean said to Melanie a little sternly. "The next time you see a loose horse galloping at you, it would be smart to step out of its way," he admonished.

Melanie looked into the man's green eyes with her own unwavering gaze. It was the same defiant look she used with Mr. Howard when she was sent to his office for causing trouble in school. "I knew he would stop," she told him. It was true. But how she had known, she couldn't say.

"Oh, you did, did you?" Mr. McLean rested his hands on his hips and gave her a skeptical look. But then he smiled and said, "Thank you for catching him."

"You're welcome," Melanie said, a little puzzled that he didn't seem angrier.

"You must be Mike and Ashleigh's niece. I'm Ian

McLean. I see you've met my son, Kevin, who ought to have remembered to introduce you," he added, giving Kevin's shoulder a push.

"Dad, this is Melanie," Kevin said dutifully.

"Hi," Melanie said.

"Well, you seem to have started off your first day with plenty of excitement," Mr. McLean said, nodding toward the black horse.

"He's beautiful," Melanie said, handing over the lead rope. She couldn't take her eyes off the horse.

"He is," Mr. McLean acknowledged. "But he's got a wild streak that I can't seem to train out of him. Still, sometimes it's that wild streak that makes a winner."

Melanie eyed the horse appreciatively. The only horses she'd ever been around were the ones at Clarebrook, and they were school horses. Their legs were bumpy and crooked, or their heads were big, or they had odd scars or strangely long backs. This horse's body was clean and beautifully proportioned. Melanie could see every well-developed muscle under his perfectly smooth skin. His black coat was so shiny that the sunlight reflected off of it.

"What kind of horse is he?" Melanie asked.

Kevin laughed. "He's a Thoroughbred, of course," he said.

"Like I'm supposed to know that?" Melanie retorted.

Kevin gave her a disbelieving look. "Whitebrook is a Thoroughbred training facility," he pointed out.

"How old is he?" Melanie asked Mr. McLean.

"He's three, and it's about time he started behaving himself better," Mr. McLean said.

"What'd you say his name was?" Melanie asked Kevin.

"Pirate Treasure," Kevin said.

"It's a cool name," Melanie said, eyeing the horse. "It suits him," she decided. "But he looks more like a pirate than a treasure," she added.

"He's by a stallion called Jolly Roger, out of a mare named Treasure Boat," Mr. McLean explained. "But I'll agree with you there. He acts more like a pirate than a treasure. This horse has got more talent than most, but he's got no idea how to use it. He's got brilliant speed, but he can turn it off as fast as he turns it on." Ian shook his head regretfully.

Melanie couldn't help smiling at Mr. McLean's description of Pirate as the big horse continued to nuzzle her hair. Already she could tell that this horse had loads of personality.

The girl who'd been riding Pirate during his gate training came slowly toward them. She was limping slightly.

"How's your seat, Naomi?" Mr. McLean called.

"It's just sore enough to make me want to get back on that rogue of a horse," she said with a laugh.

"All right then. Let's give it another try. He seems to have calmed down now," Mr. McLean said. "Oh, this is Melanie . . . ?"

"Graham," Melanie offered.

"Melanie Graham," Mr. McLean repeated. "Melanie, this is Naomi Traeger, one of our best bugs."

"Hello, Melanie," the girl said, flashing her a friendly grin. She had long dark hair gathered into a braid in back and warm brown eyes. She was as tiny as Melanie, though obviously a few years older. Sixteen, maybe, Melanie guessed.

"What's a bug?" Melanie asked.

"Oh, that just means she's not good enough to be a real jockey yet," Kevin teased.

"Enough of that, Kevin McLean," Naomi warned him. "I'll put you up on Pirate and we'll see who ends up on top," she joked.

Kevin shook his head. "I've got better sense than to ride a horse with my knees up to my ears," he told her.

"What's a bug?" Melanie repeated.

"It means I'm an apprentice jockey," Naomi explained. "When they list you on a racing form, you get an asterisk by your name as long as you're an apprentice. I guess once somebody thought the star looked like a little six-legged bug and the name just stuck."

"When do you stop being a bug?" Melanie wanted to know.

"She never stops," Kevin teased.

"When you win your first race," Naomi said, ignoring Kevin. "Give me a leg up, Ian?" she asked Mr. McLean.

He took her left leg and hoisted her into the saddle.

"Let's try it again, Pirate," Naomi said, gathering up the reins.

"I've made up my mind we're going to load this horse in the gate if it takes all day," Mr. McLean said. "Or else we're changing the horse's name to Shipwreck and sending him down the road."

He started back toward the training oval, leading Naomi, who perched placidly on top of the huge horse, bobbing in time with his languid walk. Melanie watched with admiration.

"Does he really have to go into that thing?" Melanie asked. As she watched, Mr. McLean began leading Pirate toward the gate again. "I mean, couldn't he race, anyway? He looks so fast."

"He is fast," Kevin said. "Dad thinks he's one of the most talented racers we've had here in a long time. But they all have to start from the gate. No matter how fast he is, a horse can't be in a race until it loads up quietly and the track steward gives it gate approval."

"Will your dad really get rid of the horse if he doesn't go into the gate?" Melanie asked.

"Well, Dad's pretty patient with young horses, but Pirate's been causing an awful lot of trouble lately," Kevin told her. "And if they don't get him into the gate soon, he's not going to be much good for racing. He's already missed half his three-year-old season."

Instantly Melanie's heart went out to the horse. She knew how it felt to be sent away. There was something about the horse that had caught Melanie's eye, and it wasn't just his striking good looks. She had a funny feeling that he'd sensed her there in the path before he'd seen her. Maybe that was how she'd known he would stop in front of her. Then she shook her head. What was she doing, getting so interested in a horse? She wasn't going to get attached to another horse ever again. And she certainly didn't want any of the people at White-brook to think she liked it there already.

"Come on. Christina's waiting up at the barn," Kevin said. "I'll show you around the whole place later if you want."

"Whatever," Melanie said, trying to sound bored. But she was curious to see the whole farm. Melanie glanced over her shoulder at Pirate, who was once again balking at the starting gate. Then she followed Kevin up to the stables.

"That's the stallion barn over there," Kevin was saying as they reached the top of the hill where three large red barns were arranged in a U shape. "And that's the foaling barn, where most of the mares are. And this is the training barn," he said as they went in.

Melanie stopped just inside the doorway and looked down the long center aisle, lined on either side with spacious box stalls. It seemed to go on forever. Melanie counted fourteen stalls on each side. As she followed Kevin down the aisle, she saw that only a few stalls were empty.

"How many horses do they have here?" Melanie asked.

"Well, it varies a little, depending on the time of year," Kevin explained. "Right now we have a lot, maybe fifty or sixty in all. But there's a big horse auction at Keeneland every summer and we'll sell a lot of the yearlings then."

"Oh," Melanie said absently. She walked slowly, looking from side to side. In every stall was a beautiful shiny horse—Thoroughbred, she reminded herself. Some of them put their heads over the open top doors of the stalls as she passed. Their faces were curious and friendly. Melanie couldn't help wanting to touch them, but she held back. *Don't let them think you like anything about this place,* she reminded herself. *Remember, you're going home as soon as you convince them how miserable and homesick you are.* She shoved her hands into the pockets of her jean shorts and followed Kevin down the aisle.

At the far end of the barn Melanie spotted Christina. She was brushing a tall, elegant-looking horse with a coat the color of storm clouds splotched with dapples and a dark mane and tail streaked with silver. It was one of the prettiest horses Melanie had ever seen. Instantly she was envious.

"Hi, Chris," Kevin said.

"Hi," Christina said to both of them.

"I'm going to tack up Jasper," Kevin said. "Are you almost ready?"

"Yes," Christina said. "I just have to go over her with the soft brush."

"Okay. Meet you outside in ten minutes?" he asked.

"Yep," Christina said as Kevin went back up the aisle.

"Is this your horse?" Melanie asked, her gaze fixed on the beautiful dapple gray.

"Yes," Christina answered proudly. "This is Sterling."

"Is it a boy or a girl?" Melanie asked.

"She's a mare," Christina said. "She's four years old, and we got her off the track when we were up in New York. She didn't like being a racehorse, did you, girl?" Christina said, petting the horse's neck.

Christina's tone irritated Melanie. She sounded so superior whenever she talked about horses, as if she knew so much more than Melanie. It made Melanie want to antagonize her.

"How do you know she didn't like being a racehorse?" Melanie demanded.

"Because I saw her run," Christina said as she began to go over the horse's shiny clean coat with a soft dandy brush. "Sterling was brilliant as long as she was all alone, out in front or in back, but as soon as the other horses crowded her, she would quit or run away," Christina explained. "She just hated it. I could see it in her face. Sterling's a solo performer."

"What do you mean—a solo performer?" Melanie asked.

"Well, she likes to perform, but she's better when she's in the ring all alone. We're training her to be an Event horse. Eventing is where you do jumping and dressage," Christina added.

"I know," Melanie said quickly, although she hadn't. She did know what dressage was. One of the trainers at Clarebrook taught dressage, but Melanie didn't think much of it. She'd watched a class once and thought it looked completely boring—five older women working at the sitting trot for an hour while the instructor yelled at them to put their hands down and get their horses on the bit.

"Why do you want to do dressage?" Melanie asked, letting her distaste come out in the word.

Christina gave her an uncertain look. "Well, if you do Eventing, you have to train in dressage. Of course, I like jumping better, but dressage tests are really challenging, too, in a different way. Dressage teaches you to ride correctly and it teaches your horse to respond to your aids instantly. I didn't have much patience for it at first, but I have to admit it's made me a better rider," Christina added. "Mona Gardener, my trainer, says dressage teaches the rider and the horse to think together, and then they can really work together. I think it's true."

Melanie watched as Christina began brushing the mare's forehead lovingly with a tiny, soft face brush. Sterling bowed her head and closed her eyes as Christina brushed, obviously enjoying the attention. It reminded Melanie of the way Milky Way used to like to be groomed with a hard rubber curry comb. And that reminded her that she was never going to be able to curry Milky Way again. For a moment Melanie felt the awful sadness well up in her again, and she looked around for something—anything—that would distract her.

Christina was still talking about her horse. "Sterling really seems to like the first-level dressage test we've been working on. And Mona says her extended trot is one of the most gorgeous she's ever seen."

Melanie was only half listening to Christina's chatter. She wanted to touch Sterling, to see if her coat really felt as soft and silky as it looked. Melanie reached out her left hand and was just about to stroke the horse's neck when Christina yelled, "Don't touch her!"

6

SURPRISED, MELANIE JERKED HER HAND AWAY. "WHY NOT?" she demanded, planting her hand on her hip.

"I didn't mean to yell," Christina said apologetically. "It's just that Sterling has a problem with strangers touching her."

"I've been standing right beside her for ten minutes," Melanie said. "Why would she care if I touched her? She's just a horse."

"She was abused at the racetrack," Christina told her. "Her groom used to be really rough with her." Christina's voice became low and fierce. Melanie had the feeling she was trying not to cry. "He used to beat her."

"That's terrible," Melanie said sincerely.

"I know," Christina said. "But I caught him doing it. When Sterling's owner found out about it, he fired the groom. But now she's really nervous around strangers, and sometimes she'll still bite at people. But not me. Right, Sterling?" she said in the sugary voice she seemed to always use when she was talking to the horse. "You would never bite me, would you?"

"So you're the only one who can touch her?" Melanie asked skeptically.

"Well, no, not only me. The people she's used to can handle her just fine. But you'd better not try it until you've been around her some," Christina told her.

Melanie was pretty sure Christina was just being bossy. Why would the horse stand there calmly letting Christina groom her but go crazy if Melanie touched her? Melanie didn't believe for a second that Christina's parents would let her have a horse that was dangerous. She decided that when Christina wasn't around, she would find out for herself whether the horse would really freak out if a stranger came near her.

"So are you coming riding with me and Kevin?" Christina asked. "I mean, I understand you might not want to if your arm still hurts a lot." She hesitated. "Does it?"

"Does it what?"

"Hurt a lot?"

"It always hurts," Melanie said flatly. "I told you that yesterday. But I'm used to it. It's not the worst pain I've ever felt."

Christina's hazel eyes locked with Melanie's, and Melanie knew what the girl was thinking—what did

69

it feel like to be responsible for the death of a horse? She saw the flash of shock and disapproval in her cousin's eyes. And she could tell that, like everyone else, Christina thought the accident was all Melanie's fault.

There was an uncomfortable silence before Christina spoke again. "Anyway, if you feel like coming along, you can ride Moonlight," she offered. "She's really quiet and easy to handle, and she neck reins, so you can steer her with one hand—if you're allowed to ride. Did the doctor say you could ride yet?" she asked worriedly.

Melanie bristled at that. Allowed to ride? She didn't need anyone's permission. "I can ride," Melanie said. As soon as she said it, she remembered that she had made a promise not to ride horses anymore. How could she have forgotten it so soon? She could have kicked herself. She wanted to tag along with Christina and Kevin, both because she was curious to see the whole farm and she sensed that Christina probably didn't really want her to come along. But if she rode, would she be betraying Milky Way?

Of course you would, Melanie told herself. "I just don't feel like it right now," she told Christina.

"Oh. Well, okay, if you're sure," Christina said, plainly relieved.

"I'm sure," Melanie said. Wistfully she imagined riding across all that green pasture and galloping up one of those big hills the way she used to do in Central Park. She was going to miss that.

"What are you going to do while we're out?" Christina asked. "I really have to ride Sterling. She's in training for an Event we're entering soon. Otherwise, I'd stay here with you."

"I'll be fine," Melanie said. "I'll just walk around and check out the place."

"Okay," Christina said.

"Hey, yesterday when we drove up we saw those baby horses, remember?" Melanie asked. "Where are they? Can I go see them?"

"Oh, sure you can," Christina said. "They're out in that first paddock at the top of the driveway." She pointed out the barn door. "Go straight out that way, and then to your left, and you'll see them just beyond that other barn."

"Great," Melanie said. She started to head that way.

"Um, Melanie?" Christina stopped her.

"Yeah?"

"That other barn? That's the stallion barn. I'd stay out of there if I were you. Mr. Ballard, the barn manager, isn't too crazy about people walking through. And some of the stallions are really aggressive," she added.

"Yeah, yeah," Melanie said. She turned her back on her cousin, rolling her eyes, and stepped out the door. When was the girl going to stop acting like Melanie knew nothing about horses? Now of course she would have to check out the stallion barn. She wasn't about to let Christina boss her around like that.

Melanie waited just outside the barn until Kevin and Christina had mounted up. "Have a good ride," she told them.

"See you later," Kevin said cheerfully.

"Remember what I told you about the stallions," Christina warned.

"Oh, I will," Melanie said in a good-little-girl voice. With a wave she started toward the driveway. She pretended to be following Christina's directions to the paddock where the foals were turned out, but as soon as Christina and Kevin had ridden out of sight beyond the stables, Melanie turned and headed straight for the stallion barn. She would have plenty of time to see the foals later, she told herself.

The inside of the stallion barn looked pretty much like the training barn, as far as Melanie could tell, except that the stalls were bigger. Melanie peered into the first stall on the right. In it was a big black stallion. "Blues King," Melanie read aloud from the plaque nailed to the door of the stall. The big horse was looking out the window of his stall. When he heard Melanie's voice, he swung his head around and peered at her. Then he turned and stepped toward her. The expression in his eyes was kind and inquisitive.

Melanie looked around carefully to be sure no one was watching, then undid the latch that held the top half of the stall door and swung it open. The stallion immediately put his head over the top of the door. Melanie reached up and began scratching his massive cheeks. He lowered his head and leaned into her hands, encouraging her to scratch harder.

Melanie smiled. It always amazed her that such a huge animal could behave just like a big pet. "You like that, huh?" she murmured, going over and over the sides of his face with her fingers.

As if he were answering her, the big horse gave a soft, low nicker. Melanie laughed. "Oh, you stallions— you're so aggressive and mean," she said. She spent a few more moments with the horse, then gently pushed his head back so that she could close the door. "See you around," she said.

For a moment the stallion looked at her wistfully, then turned around and began gazing out the window again. Melanie watched him for a moment, then wandered on through the barn, curious to see the rest of the stallions.

She stepped down the aisle, reading the names of the stallions on the plaques nailed to the door of each stall: "Wonder's Pride, Saturday Affair, Make It So." Melanie murmured the names aloud to herself as she gazed at the stallions. Some of them pawed or snorted at her as she passed by. One stallion in particular caught her eye and she stopped to get a better look at him. He was dark gray with black markings like eyebrows over his eyes that gave him an intense expression.

"The Terminator." Melanie read his name out. As she spoke, the stallion tossed his head, then stood perfectly still, gazing intently at Melanie.

Melanie was mesmerized by the gray stallion. He wasn't as big as the other studs, but he had a fierce, independent look about him. Melanie decided she wanted to pet him. She undid the latches on the top and bottom of the door, and went into the stall.

"Here, boy," Melanie said, holding out a hand as if she had a treat for him. "Come here." She stepped slowly toward him, her eyes locked with his. "Don't be afraid."

The stallion kept staring at her as she drew nearer. The only thing moving was his nostrils, which flared wide with each breath he drew, showing the bright pink lining inside. Melanie was nearly hypnotized by the horse's eyes, which were so dark they were almost black. She could see her own outstretched hand reflected in them as she got closer and closer. Something about the horse was wildly beautiful, like moonlight or mountains. Melanie wished she had her sketchbook with her. She wanted to draw the stallion's stunning head. "I wonder why they call you The Terminator," Melanie mused.

Her fingertips were just inches from his velvety muzzle when suddenly the stallion let out a scream of defiance and lunged at her. With a shocked gasp, Melanie leaped backward, tripped over her own feet, and fell out the stall door, landing hard on her left side. She lay there for a moment, stunned. The other stallions had become agitated at the disturbance. They snorted and stamped, and one of them let out a challenging whinny. The Terminator stood in the open doorway of his stall, glaring menacingly at Melanie. She got one look at his terrifying face, ears laid back, teeth bared angrily, before he lowered his head and prepared to charge her again.

Melanie wondered for a split second what the stallion would do to her if he caught her, but she didn't wait to find out. She scrambled to her feet and bolted for the door as fast as she could run.

"Hey, what are you doing in here?" a man shouted angrily behind her. But she didn't stop to answer him. She heard the clatter of a horse's hooves on the concrete floor of the barn and ran faster, terrified that The Terminator would follow her. Fearfully she glanced over her shoulder, certain she was going to see his dark diabolical face with those big flaring nostrils charging up behind her. Then while she was looking back, she ran right into something.

"*Aaah!*" Melanie screamed before she could stop herself. She reeled backward and tripped again.

"Melanie!" It was her Uncle Mike. He grabbed her and kept her from falling down. "What's the matter?" he asked her, sounding full of concern.

"I—I—" Melanie was still panting from her fright and from the run.

"Are you all right?" Uncle Mike asked her.

Melanie nodded. "I'm fine," she managed to get out.

"What happened? What are you running from?" he asked.

Melanie didn't answer. Should she tell him? Christina had told her to stay out of the stallion barn. Would she get in big trouble if they found out she had let the stallion loose? She decided to play dumb. After all, she was from New York City. They wouldn't expect her to know much about horses. Quickly she worked up a few tears and blurted out a story.

"Oh, Uncle Mike, I was so scared. I was walking through that barn over there, looking around, and I wanted to pet this horse because I thought he was so pretty. I didn't think you would mind," she added conscientiously. "So I opened the door to reach in and he just attacked me," Melanie said. "He tried to bite me and he chased me out of the barn. I thought he was going to kill me," she said dramatically. "That horse is dangerous!"

She watched Uncle Mike's face as he listened to the story. She was pretty sure he was buying it.

"Melanie, I'm sorry you were frightened, but you mustn't go into the horses' stalls without permission," he said sternly. "You don't know anything about stallions, I know, but they can be aggressive. You could have really been hurt."

"Well, we don't have horses like that in New York," Melanie said. "I didn't know."

His tone softened. "I know you didn't," he said. "But from now on, you let the stallions alone, all right?"

Melanie nodded and glanced uneasily back up at the stallion barn. She hoped The Terminator wasn't still loose. Then she saw a man come out of the barn and look around sharply. When he saw her and Mike, he strode down the hill, a purposeful frown on his face. Melanie judged him to be in his late forties or maybe fifty. He was short but sturdily built, with thinning gray hair and a no-nonsense air about him. Melanie disliked him instantly. He reminded her of the headmaster at her school in New York.

"Hello, George," Uncle Mike said pleasantly. "I understand The Terminator got loose. Did you catch him all right?"

The man ignored him. "You're the one that let my stud out, aren't you?" he said to Melanie. "You stay out of my barn, you hear?"

Melanie bristled. "It's not your barn," she retorted. "Is it, Uncle Mike?"

"George, this is my niece, Melanie," Uncle Mike said. "Melanie, this is Mr. Ballard. He manages the stallion barn here at Whitebrook."

"And I don't allow kids wandering through the barn," Mr. Ballard asserted.

"She didn't know anything about the stallions," Uncle Mike said soothingly. "Did you, Mel?"

Melanie shook her head innocently.

"All the more reason to keep away from them!" Mr. Ballard grumbled. "Now see that you do!" He glared at Melanie to make the point. "Mike," he nodded politely to her uncle. Then he turned and stalked back up the path. Melanie stuck out her tongue at him. She would keep away from The Terminator for sure, but he couldn't make her stay away from any of the other horses.

"Don't worry about him, Mel," Uncle Mike told her when Mr. Ballard was out of earshot. "He's all bark and no bite. But stay out of the stallion barn from now on, unless you're with me. By the way—where's Christina?" he asked.

Melanie shrugged her good shoulder. "She went for a ride."

Uncle Mike sighed. "Didn't you want to go? Did she show you old Moonlight?"

"Yeah, yeah," Melanie said. "I didn't feel like riding, okay?"

Uncle Mike gave her the deeply concerned adult look that made Melanie nauseous. *You think you know so much about me,* she thought. *But you don't know anything.*

"How's the shoulder?" he asked her.

"Fine," Melanie said flatly.

"You know, everybody falls off sometimes," Uncle Mike told her.

"Yeah, so?"

"So, I know you haven't been back on a horse since your accident," he went on. "And I think—"

"I can't ride with a dislocated shoulder," Melanie interrupted him. She didn't want to tell him the real reason she wasn't going to ride. And it wasn't just for Milky Way's sake. She had begun to realize it as she watched Kevin and Christina on their horses. It was a terrible, uncomfortable feeling that she had never experienced before, and the more she thought about it, the more she didn't want to face it. But she knew what it was: fear.

"I think you should give it a try soon," Uncle Mike went on smoothly. "It'll give you back your confidence. You know, I've had some really bad falls, and some injuries here and there, but I learned that the quicker I got back on a horse and rode again, the easier it got to bounce back from those falls." He gazed at her earnestly with his blue eyes.

Melanie stared back at him. "I don't intend to ride again," she said quietly. "And you can't make me." She sent him a piercing look, then turned and walked away.

Melanie's heart was pounding as she walked, and her hands were clenched into angry fists by her sides. *Stupid*, she thought. *Do you think it's so easy to just climb back on any old horse after an accident like that?* But deep down, she knew, she wasn't really angry at her uncle. Melanie was angry at herself.

She wasn't sure which direction she was headed, but after walking for a few minutes she found herself approaching the training oval. She spotted Mr. McLean and realized that he was still working with the horse called Pirate Treasure. Naomi was still in the saddle, and she and Mr. McLean were trying to get Pirate to walk quietly into the starting gate. There was an oak tree near the track where the starting gate was set up. Melanie sat down in the shade and began to watch.

"Come on, now," Mr. McLean urged the horse. He made an encouraging clucking sound as he led him up to the gate.

The horse came along willingly until he almost had his head in the gate, but then he balked and refused to take another step forward.

"Come on, Pirate," Naomi coaxed him. "Walk on."

The horse started to take another step. Melanie thought he was about to walk in, but again, as soon as his head was almost in the starting gate, he gave a nervous snort, threw his head up, and backed up rapidly. On his next approach, he repeated the behavior, throwing in a couple of bucks for good measure. Melanie watched Naomi keenly to see if Pirate would get her off again, but the girl stayed calmly stuck to the saddle no matter what the horse did.

"Come on, Pirate," Melanie said softly. "All you have to do is take one more step forward and you'll be inside. Then you can race." But no matter how Mr. McLean and Naomi coaxed him, Pirate refused to go into the starting gate.

They worked with the horse for the next half hour, until the sun had crept overhead and the shadow of the oak tree fell behind Melanie. The horse had long since stopped rearing, bucking, or backing up. He simply planted his feet and refused to budge as soon as they had his head in the gate. "You're about as stubborn as me," Melanie murmured. The more defiant the horse was, the more Melanie wanted to try getting him in herself. At last Melanie stood up and walked over to the fence rail.

Mr. McLean put his hands on his hips and stared at the dirt. Then he took a deep breath. "I'm giving him one more chance, and if he won't walk in, I don't know what else to do."

"Mr. McLean?" Melanie said quietly. "Can I try leading him into the gate?"

7

MR. MCLEAN AND NAOMI BOTH LOOKED AT MELANIE. THEN they looked at each other. "He let her catch him when he got loose earlier," Naomi reminded Mr. McLean. "Usually he won't come near anybody when he's loose—you know how he is."

Mr. McLean seemed hesitant. "Weeell," he said, lifting his cap and wiping the sweat off his forehead before he settled it back on his head. "I don't usually like to let anyone outside my staff handle the horses."

"Come on, Ian. Let her try," Naomi said. "What could it hurt? He's not going to break loose again."

"All right, all right," Mr. McLean agreed. "We've nothing to lose, that's for sure." He looked sharply at Melanie. "Do you know how to handle horses safely from the ground?"

Melanie nodded. She climbed over the fence into the

82

training track while Mr. McLean led the horse around in a small circle. He faced the gate and handed the lead line out to Melanie.

"If he rears, you let go, you hear? I don't want you getting hurt," Mr. McLean warned her.

"He won't rear," Melanie assured him. Somehow she just knew the horse wasn't going to try anything with her leading him.

She crossed the track and took the lead line from Mr. McLean. "Hi, Pirate," Melanie greeted him, patting his muscular shoulder. The horse bent his head around to snuffle at her. Melanie could have sworn he recognized her from the morning because he nuzzled her hair again in the same way, then put his head down and seemed to sigh with relief. "Ready, smart boy?" Melanie asked him.

She took up the lead line in her good left hand and started forward. Secretly she crossed her fingers on her right hand. "Come on, Pirate," she whispered to him. "Let's walk right into that gate. You can do it." The horse's shiny black coat glinted in the bright sunlight as he stepped along willingly by Melanie's side.

As they reached the gate, Pirate's head went up and he began to prance nervously. "Get up there, Pirate," Naomi said when the horse hesitated.

Pirate's ears were pointed forward alertly. He acted as if he were going to balk again. "Come on, Pirate. Let's go," Melanie said in a soft, encouraging voice. They were just a couple of feet from the starting gate.

Melanie could sense that the horse trusted her, though she couldn't explain it. And although she'd seen him acting up with the adults when they handled him, she was quietly confident that he would behave with her. She held her breath and kept walking forward, hoping the horse would simply follow her. Miraculously, he did.

Ian McLean gave a soft whistle of appreciation as Pirate walked calmly into the gate and stood quietly next to Melanie. Naomi smiled broadly and patted the horse's neck. "Good boy," she said heartily.

"Good boy," Melanie echoed, letting out her breath in a relieved sigh. She was delighted that she had been the one who finally got Pirate into the gate.

"Well, now, what do you think made the difference?" Mr. McLean asked Naomi.

"I have no idea," she said. "I guess he must have just decided he was ready. Or he's decided he likes Melanie," Naomi said, winking at Melanie.

"Well, let's work him through it a few more times, as long as we've got him going," Mr. McLean said. "Melanie, would you mind doing that again?" he asked.

Melanie led the horse forward out of the gate and circled him around. Then she approached the gate again. The horse walked right in again, as if he'd been doing it all his life.

"Close the back, Joe," Mr. McLean said to a groom who had been standing by. Joe Kisner, Pirate's groom, walked over and closed the gate behind Pirate. It made a clanking sound, but the horse didn't move.

"Good boy, Pirate," Naomi said again. "I think he's going to be okay, Ian," she told Mr. McLean happily.

"What a relief," Mr. McLean said. "I thought we were never going to be able to race this horse, the way he's been acting. Thank goodness he's finally settled down with the gate. Still, I can't see what's made the difference." He shrugged. "Let's try it a few more times. If he's good, tomorrow we'll get the track steward out here to approve him."

Melanie brought Pirate into the gate several more times. The last few times Mr. McLean had Joe shut the front first and then the back so that the horse was completely enclosed. But it didn't seem to bother him.

"Well, I guess that's enough for today," Mr. McLean said with a glance upward. The sky had become overcast and the air was heavy, threatening rain. "You can take him up now, Joe," he said to the groom.

Naomi hopped down from Pirate's back. Joe was about to take the horse when Melanie spoke up. "Can I take him up to the barn?"

"I don't see why not," Mr. McLean said. "You've certainly handled him more successfully than any of the rest of us."

Melanie smiled and took the reins from Joe. "Where does he live?" she asked.

"Go along with her, Joe, and show her where to put him," Mr. McLean told the groom.

"This way," Joe said, starting up the path toward the training barn.

Joe showed Melanie where Pirate's stall was. He let Melanie put the horse on crossties and brush him off. Melanie spent a long time going over and over Pirate's coal black coat with a dandy brush, until every sweat mark from the saddle was gone. She had forgotten how she loved grooming horses. When Pirate's body was as soft and shiny as black velvet, she went to work on his face with a rub rag. She rubbed at the sweat marks from the bridle and Pirate lowered his head and leaned into her hand. When she stopped for a moment to rest her arm, Pirate put his muzzle against Melanie's ear and delicately lipped a lock of Melanie's hair.

"None of that now," she chided him. "Just because I'm brushing you doesn't mean I like you or anything. I'm not really planning to stay involved with horses."

Pirate sighed deeply and pushed his face into Melanie's chest. Then he closed his eyes and simply hung his head there, as if all he wanted were to be close to her. Pirate had chosen her, Melanie was sure, because he was like her—he didn't fit into everyone's plan. Why else would he let her lead him into the gate after the adults had tried for hours and failed to get him in? And why had he stopped and come straight to her in the path when he got loose that morning?

"But I didn't choose you, you hear?" she told the

horse. "I just wanted to help you out with that gate thing."

"That was a great gallop, wasn't it?"

Melanie heard the sound of horses' feet clopping on the concrete floor of the barn and recognized Christina's voice. She quickly took a step back from Pirate, then picked up the brush and began to go over his neck with it again, although the horse couldn't have been any cleaner.

"That was fun," Kevin was saying as he led his honey-colored horse, Jasper, into the barn. "But I still say I would've beaten you if Jasper hadn't stumbled."

Christina was right behind him leading Sterling. "In your dreams, McLean," she said with a big grin. "Sterling can outrun Jasper any day and you know it. An Arab's no match for a Thoroughbred."

"He's an Anglo-Arab," Kevin retorted. "He's half Thoroughbred, anyway. And he got the best half, if you ask me. Thoroughbreds are too stubborn."

"They are not," Christina said indignantly. Just then Sterling stopped. "Come on, Sterling," Christina said, moving to lead her forward again. But the mare didn't budge. She tugged harder on the reins and clucked. Sterling didn't move. "Sterling, come on," Christina said.

Kevin looked back and laughed when he saw what was happening. "Oh no, they're not stubborn, not one little bit," he kidded her.

Christina was still tugging on the reins, trying to get

Sterling to walk forward. The mare's ears were pointed alertly down the aisle and she let out a little squeal. Christina laughed. "What's she looking at, I wonder?"

Then Pirate let out a low whinny that shook his whole body. He lifted one front foot and struck at the floor, sending sparks from his metal shoe.

"Oh!" Melanie said, startled. Pirate had almost stomped her foot when he struck. She managed to get it out of the way just in time.

"Hey, what're you doing with that horse?" Christina said.

"Nothing," Melanie replied. She stepped back. "I was just brushing him off."

"Does Ian know you took him out?" Christina said suspiciously.

"I didn't take him out," Melanie objected. "I'm putting him away."

"It's all right, Christina," Ian McLean said. He had just come into the barn. "I told Melanie she could put the horse away."

At that moment, Pirate lunged forward, breaking his crossties.

"Pirate!" Melanie said, starting after him. She grabbed one of the trailing crossties and tried to stop him, but he kept going toward Sterling, dragging Melanie along with him.

"Keep him away," Christina yelled as the big black horse trotted up to Sterling.

"I'm trying," Melanie hissed, planting her feet and

pulling back on the crosstie with all the strength in her good arm. But she couldn't stop him. Her feet slid on the concrete floor as Pirate dragged her down the aisle. "Whoa, Pirate," Melanie commanded, but it was useless. Pirate and Sterling were intent on one thing: each other.

"Hey!" Kevin protested as Pirate slammed right into Jasper on his way. Jasper, much smaller and lighter, took a good bump from Pirate. But not to be outdone, he wheeled around and kicked out indignantly with both hind legs before Kevin could do anything to stop him.

"Ow!" Melanie said as one of Jasper's hooves struck her a glancing blow in the hip. His other hoof connected squarely with Pirate's shoulder, but it may as well have been a fly biting him. Pirate barely noticed. He just kept barreling down the aisle toward Sterling.

Kevin managed to get Jasper into his stall. He quickly closed the door and grabbed a lead shank hanging on a stall door nearby.

Pirate reached the mare. Sterling began switching her tail, and the two horses blew into each other's nostrils. Then Pirate struck out again with a forefoot. He lifted it high, catching Sterling's shoulder. Melanie saw that the blow had opened up a gash that quickly began to drip blood.

"Oh no! Get him—get him away from her!" Christina wailed.

Melanie tried hard to pull Pirate's head away, but

Ian pushed her aside. "Get out of the way, Melanie," he said, grabbing the horse by the halter. "Joe!" he called. "Maureen! Somebody, bring me a lead shank. Christina, turn your mare around and get her out of here, quick," he ordered.

Christina yanked Sterling's head away from Pirate's and turned the mare around. Reluctantly Sterling followed. Kevin handed his father the lead shank, which Mr. McLean quickly clipped onto Pirate's halter, expertly drawing the chain across the horse's nose. Melanie knew that the chain would give him more control over the horse if he resisted, but she winced when Mr. McLean gave it a firm snatch to get the horse's attention off Christina's mare.

In a moment he had Pirate in his stall. Melanie stood back against the wall, rubbing at her hip. Pirate began circling his stall nervously. Melanie looked around defensively. Was everyone going to blame the incident on her? Why couldn't she do anything right? And what would they do to Pirate?

8

KEVIN WAS LOOKING AT HER WITH CONCERN. HE WENT OVER and stood beside her. "I'm sorry Jasper kicked you. Are you okay?" he asked her.

Melanie nodded, still rubbing her hip. She had never been kicked by a horse and was surprised at how much it had hurt. It was about the same as getting whacked with a baseball bat. But already the pain was starting to subside. She was pretty sure she would have a bad bruise but nothing more.

"Ian? Can I bring Sterling in now?" Christina called anxiously from outside the barn.

"Sure. Come on in. Let me take a look at that shoulder," Ian said.

Christina brought Sterling back inside and they all went to look at her shoulder. Pirate's hoof had opened up a one-inch gash that was still dripping blood. Melanie shuddered and looked away.

"What do you think, Ian? Is it bad?" Christina asked.

Mr. McLean gently examined the cut. "Don't you worry, Chris. It's not too bad. But I do think it needs a stitch or two."

"Stitches?" Christina wailed. "Oh no!"

"Now, now," Mr. McLean said soothingly. "I've seen horses hurt themselves worse than that in turnout. It's not bad. We just don't want a scar. Dr. Lanum will come out and fix her right up."

"Dad, what do you think made Pirate act like that?" Kevin asked.

"It wasn't just Pirate," Melanie pointed out.

"Yes it was," Christina said angrily. "That horse is a maniac. He always has been. You shouldn't have had him out like that," she accused.

"I told you, I didn't take him out," Melanie retorted. "I was putting him away. Anyway, it's not my fault if you can't handle your own horse." Melanie's heart pounded with anger and she was shaking. Why was it always her fault? Why was everything always her fault?

"Kevin, go and find Maureen, would you?" Mr. McLean said smoothly. "I think she's in the office. And ask her to call Dr. Lanum to come out and stitch this horse's shoulder," he directed. "Christina, untack your mare and put a halter on her."

Kevin went to find Maureen Mack, the assistant trainer. Christina looped an elbow through Sterling's reins and started to unbuckle the girth.

"I'll hold her for you," Melanie offered, trying to be helpful. She started to put a hand on Sterling's reins, but when she did the horse pinned her ears and tried to bite her.

"Hey!" Melanie said, jerking her hand back just in time.

"Just stay away from her," Christina snapped. "I told you she's uncomfortable around strangers."

"Christina," Mr. McLean warned.

Melanie didn't wait to hear Christina's response. She turned around and ran out of the barn all the way back to the house. She was angry at her cousin for blaming Pirate's behavior on her. And she didn't understand why she kept getting into trouble with horses. She had only been brushing Pirate. It wasn't her fault he broke the crossties.

All she wanted to do was hide, or better still, disappear. She stumbled into the kitchen and up the stairs to her room but stopped herself in the doorway. It wasn't her room. Her room was back in New York, along with everything else that was safe and familiar to her. Melanie backed out of the doorway and went back down the hall. Beside the bathroom was another door. Melanie opened it and found a rickety flight of stairs that she realized must lead to an attic.

Good, Melanie thought. An attic was just space. It wasn't the same as her own room, but it wasn't anyone else's room, either. She ducked into her aunt and uncle's room and grabbed the cordless phone, then headed up to the attic.

Melanie reached the top of the creaky stairs and stepped into a little attic room cheerfully lit by two dormer windows. There were the usual boxes and unused or broken pieces of furniture. Under one of the windows was an old leather chair with a soft and thread-bare quilt draped over one arm. Melanie went to the chair and curled up in it. Drawing her knees up to her chin, she wrapped her good arm around them and rested her head against the cracked leather back of the chair.

Melanie's dad had left for Europe the same day he put Melanie on the plane to New York. Melanie had barely spoken to her father in the week following the accident because she'd been so upset with him for making her go to Kentucky. She dug into her pocket and found the number of her father's hotel in Munich. Melanie wondered for a second what time it was in Germany but decided it didn't matter. She had to talk to her father. She had been in Kentucky less than twenty-four hours and already everyone was blaming things on her. She had to get away from this place where no one trusted her or liked her. She was positive that when her dad heard how bad she felt, he would let her come back to New York. Maybe he'd even send her a ticket to join him in Europe.

She dialed the complicated series of numbers and eventually heard a man's voice answer, "Hotel Platzl."

"Room four-twenty, please," Melanie said. She held

her breath, hoping her father would pick up the phone. After a few rings, he did.

"Dad!" Melanie said with relief.

"Melanie?" her father sounded surprised. "What's the matter, honey?"

"Dad," Melanie said. "This place is awful! You wouldn't believe what just happened. This horse attacked another horse and they said it was my fault!"

"Whoa, whoa! What are you talking about? Attacking horses? You're not hurt, are you?"

"No," Melanie said. "Dad, please get me out of here. I have to get out of here!" Melanie had been trying to keep her voice level, but she could hear herself starting to sound frantic. "Everyone hates me. Please, please let me go back to New York. I won't get in any trouble ever again. Or let me come to Europe with you," she pleaded. "Please, Dad." There was a long silence at the other end of the phone. "Dad?" Melanie said.

"Melanie, we've been over and over this," her dad said. "Don't you think you're being a little unreasonable? You've hardly been there a day. Come on. Give it a chance. Things will settle down and you'll get used to it. You just need a little time to adjust. And I know no one hates you," he said firmly.

"But, Dad, you don't understand," Melanie wailed. "I have to—" She broke off, listening. Her dad had covered the mouthpiece and was saying something to someone else in the room. "Dad? Are you listening?"

"Yes, Melanie."

"Who are you talking to?" she asked.

"Susan."

Melanie felt as if someone had kicked her in the stomach. How could her dad be talking to someone else while his very own daughter was telling him how unhappy she was?

"Melanie, listen," her dad said. "I have to go. I'll call you in a couple of days. All right?"

"Whatever," Melanie said quietly.

"Promise me you'll give it a chance?"

"Sure."

"I love you, Mel," her dad said. "I'll talk to you soon, okay?"

"Bye," Melanie said, her voice almost a whisper. She heard the click as her dad hung up the phone. How could he have done this to her? She would never forgive him.

For a moment she held the phone, trying to think what to do. Then quickly she dialed a number in New York.

"Hello?" a woman's voice answered.

"Hi—is Aynslee there?" she asked.

It was a huge relief when a moment later she heard Aynslee's familiar voice on the other end of the phone. "Aynslee? It's Melanie," she said.

"Oh," Aynslee said. "Hi."

Why did she sound so stiff? "Ayns, you wouldn't believe how horrible this place is. I just had to talk to you," Melanie said.

"Well, what do you want?" Aynslee said.

Melanie froze. What did she want? Aynslee was supposed to be her best friend. Why was she acting like that? Maybe she was just hearing her wrong. "Hey, Ayns, what's the deal?" Melanie asked. "It's me, Melanie, your best friend. Remember?"

"Look, I can't really talk right now," Aynslee said.

"What do you mean? Should I call back later?"

"No. I'm not supposed to talk to you anymore," Aynslee said coolly. "My parents said. Because of the accident and sneaking out the horses and stuff."

"What?" Melanie was shocked. "What do you mean? You were in it just as much as I was!"

"Oh no I wasn't," Aynslee said. "It was your idea. Remember? I just came along because you made me."

"I made you? What are you talking about? I tried to get you not to go. Remember? How can you say I made you?" Melanie protested.

"Look, I have to go," Aynslee said.

"Aynslee, look. Let's just forget you said that, okay?" Melanie pleaded. She was beginning to panic. First her father had no time for her. Then her best friend was suddenly not allowed to speak to her, and she didn't even seem to care.

"Okay. Just forget we ever spoke, okay?" Aynslee said.

"Aynslee! Why are you doing this to me?" Melanie said. "Whatever I did, I'm sorry. Tell me what I did."

"I have to go now," Aysnlee said. "Good-bye."

"Aynslee!" Melanie said. "Aynslee?"

She heard the click as Aynslee hung up. Melanie stared at the cordless phone in disbelief, then threw it into a corner of the attic. She had never felt so completely alone in her whole life. "How am I ever going to make it through this summer?" she said. Then she buried her face in the soft old quilt and sobbed.

9

A FEW DAYS LATER MELANIE WAS SITTING IN THE GRASS BY one of the paddocks. She was sketching one of the foals who'd been curious enough to stay close to her, when Ian McLean came striding toward her with his purposeful walk.

"Hello, Melanie," Mr. McLean said. He stopped near her and stood with his arms folded on the top fence rail.

"Hi," Melanie responded. The foal chose that moment to squeal and dart away to play with the other foals.

"That's a good likeness," Mr. McLean said, looking over Melanie's shoulder at the drawing of the foal.

"Thanks," Melanie said. She closed the sketchbook, feeling a little embarrassed. She didn't usually like to show people her drawings, though when she did, people always said they were good.

"I've got a proposal for you," Mr. McLean said. He was the sort of person who got right to the point, which Melanie appreciated. But the word *proposal* sounded suspicious to her.

"What is it?" she said warily.

"I need an assistant groom. One of my regular grooms, Joe Kisner, is out of town for a couple of weeks. I'm running a horse at Keeneland next week and I need an assistant groom. Naomi can handle most of it—she's riding the horse—but she'll need a helper. Can you do it?" he asked.

"Who's the horse?" Melanie asked.

Mr. McLean lifted his cap and smoothed his wavy auburn hair. He settled his cap back on his head before answering. "It's Pirate Treasure."

Melanie had just opened her mouth to say no, but before she could answer Mr. McLean went on smoothly. "Ordinarily I wouldn't be asking a kid like you to handle such a horse. It's just that I'm really stuck with Joe away and I know how good you are with Pirate. I know he trusts you. And I trust you." He paused, letting his words sink in.

Melanie thought of Pirate and how good she had felt when she had handled him. She was wary about getting too involved with him, but maybe just being his groom would be okay.

Then Melanie thought of something. "I bet my aunt and uncle won't let me," she told him.

"Yes, they will," Mr. McLean said. "I've already

spoken to your uncle. I told him I think you're big enough for the job and that Pirate thinks the same. Your uncle discussed it with your aunt on the phone and they've agreed to let you try it."

"Okay, then," Melanie said.

"I'll expect to see you in the training barn at six tomorrow morning," Mr. McLean said.

Melanie groaned inwardly at the thought of getting up so early. "I'll be there," she promised.

"Good," Mr. McLean said.

"Mr. McLean?"

"Call me Ian."

Melanie nodded. "Ian. When's the race?"

"A week from Saturday," he said.

It wasn't as hard as Melanie had thought it would be to get up the next morning. A horse was counting on her. Pirate seemed to remember her. He nickered to her when she came into his stall and eagerly pushed his face at her chest.

"Now, don't go getting all mushy on me," Melanie warned the horse. "I'm just going to be your groom for a while, until Joe gets back."

"Hi, Melanie," Naomi said. "I hear you're going to help us out with Pirate while Joe's away."

"Yeah, I guess so," Melanie said. "So, what do I do first here—feed him?"

"Nope," Naomi said. "Ian doesn't believe in having

horses run on a full belly. And they all have different styles of eating. Some like to gobble down their grain and some nibble on it for hours. He works them out first. Then after they're cooled out and are put away, they get their breakfast. That way they can eat at their own pace."

"That's pretty smart," Melanie said. "So what do I do?"

"You can start by grooming him. Then I'll show you how to put on the exercise saddle," Naomi told her.

Pirate stood quietly while Melanie worked on getting him shiny clean. When she put the exercise saddle on him, he began to perk up. By the time she had helped Naomi mount up, Pirate's head was up and he pranced grandly down to the training track.

Naomi laughed and patted Pirate's neck as they approached the dirt oval. "This horse loves to run. That's for sure," she told Melanie, who was walking down beside her. "Just look at him. The closer we get to the track, the happier he gets. And wait'll you see him run—he just tears up the track. It's funny—I've ridden a lot of different types of horses. Some of them are just doing their job. Some of them try their hearts out and never amount to much. Some are lazy and some get bored or distracted. This horse loves to fly. He can't stand the dirt in his face when another horse gets in front of him, but instead of backing off, like some horses, he digs in and runs harder until he's past. Then he stays in the front all the way. He's just amazing," Naomi said.

Melanie almost didn't want to watch Pirate's work-out. She was a little nervous that something might happen just because she was around. But nothing happened. Pirate ran fine.

"That's a black letter time, Naomi," Ian said with a smile after she had galloped him out and brought him back to a walk. "That horse is running better every day."

"Where's my groom?" Naomi asked. "Where's Mel?"

"Right here," Melanie said.

"So you take the horse and hose him off. You know how to do that?"

Melanie nodded.

Naomi went on. "Then you walk him out until he's dry. You brush him and put him in his stall. I'll show you how to mix his feed. Make sure his water buckets are clean and full," Naomi told her, hopping off Pirate and handing Melanie the reins. "I've got two more horses to ride. Then I'll come up and help you out, okay?"

"Okay. Come on, Pirate," she said, giving him a gentle tug on the reins. The big horse moved off beside her.

Back at the barn, Melanie untacked Pirate and hosed him off. Then she took him out to a grassy area just outside the barn and let him graze while she waited for him to dry. She sat on a bench, enjoying the rest after a morning of hard work, while the colt munched at the juicy grass. It felt so nice there that Melanie closed her eyes for a moment. A whiff of warm grassy breath in her face made her open them.

Pirate had walked over to Melanie and had his face right in hers. Melanie gazed into the horse's huge brown eyes. "What do you want?" she asked him.

The horse put his whole head against her chest and sighed, as if he were just glad to be near her. Melanie felt her heart quirk strangely when he did that.

"I don't fall in love with horses anymore, you know," she told him. "I'm only taking care of you to help out Ian."

Pirate began to nibble gently at Melanie's hair. Melanie couldn't resist stroking the colt's silky neck. Milky Way had never been affectionate like that, but she'd loved him, anyway. Abruptly she took her hand away. What was she doing, getting all mushy over a horse? Probably they would just end up sending him away, anyway. Or something bad would happen and she'd lose him, just like she'd lost everything else she loved.

Melanie pushed the horse's head away and stood up. "Come on. It's time to eat," she said. She tugged on the lead rope and Pirate followed her amiably back to the barn.

The rest of the week Melanie was at the barn by six o'clock every morning. It was hard work being a groom, especially with one arm, but Melanie decided she liked it. The best thing about it was that Ian treated her exactly like he treated the other grooms. It made Melanie feel very professional and very grown up.

The weather stayed muggy and overcast all week, but it didn't rain. Pirate's workout times were getting faster every day. Ian was pleased with how the colt had been running. Everything was going smoothly.

At the end of the week the sky finally broke loose with a huge thunderstorm. Melanie lay in her bed and listened to the crashes of thunder. She found herself wondering if Pirate was all right.

Melanie got up and tiptoed downstairs. She got as far as putting on an old raincoat of her uncle's she found in the mudroom before she stopped herself. What was she doing? She was only Pirate's groom, nothing more. Pirate didn't mean anything to her. He was just another horse. She took off the raincoat and went back up to her room.

The weather was perfectly clear and sunny the next morning. Everything was dripping and soggy as Melanie accompanied Pirate and Naomi down to the training oval. But the rain had cooled things off a little and the air smelled fresh.

Pirate seemed full of energy. He pranced and snorted more than usual on his way down to the ring.

"Pirate's going to run with other horses today and we're going to show them who's a winner. Right, Pirate?" Naomi smiled and gave the horse several affectionate slaps on the neck.

Pirate tossed his head playfully and pranced out to

the starting gate. He hadn't given them any more trouble at the gate since the day Melanie got him to go in. Melanie sat quietly, admiring the horse's sleek, muscular body as he jogged along.

Four other horses were also out on the track. Melanie recognized one of them: a chestnut filly called Faith that she'd seen in the training barn. The other three she didn't know.

The horses loaded up into the gate. Then the start bell rang out in the quiet morning, and with a sudden thunder of hooves the five horses took off down the dirt track. Pirate was in the lead from the start and he kept it all the way. Melanie watched, fascinated, as the horses came around the turn and flashed past her where she sat. She saw Naomi glance back to see where the rest of the pack was and then smile when she saw that the next was Faith—and she was a good four lengths behind.

In spite of her determination not to be involved, Melanie couldn't help rooting for Pirate. Clearly the horse loved to run. Melanie could see it in his face. It was impossible not to get caught up in his intensity. She jumped to her feet to get a better view. "Come on, Pirate! Go!" she cheered softly.

"It's exciting, isn't it?"

Melanie glanced up and saw her Aunt Ashleigh standing beside her. Ashleigh had come back from New Jersey just the day before. Her dark hair was pushed back with a headband, and her hazel eyes were deep and searching. Melanie avoided looking into them because when she did she had the odd sensation that Aunt Ashleigh could somehow read her thoughts.

"I guess so," Melanie said guardedly. She turned her attention back to the horses that were just a few lengths from the finish.

In the couple of seconds she'd looked away, Faith had closed on Pirate. The filly was now less than two lengths from the big black colt. But Pirate was going to win—Melanie was sure of it.

Then, just a nose from the finish line, Pirate suddenly launched himself into the air with a strange twist of his hindquarters. He came down crooked and slammed into Faith, knocking the smaller horse sideways.

"Oh!" Melanie gasped, jumping to her feet.

Faith's jockey, Anna Simms, fell off right in front of Pirate. The horse tripped over the downed girl with his front legs, then caught her squarely with a hind foot as he scrambled to keep his balance. The force of it flipped Anna over a couple of times before she came to rest in the dirt.

"What happened?" Melanie asked anxiously.

But Ashleigh had run to Anna's side. The girl was still down, lying in the dirt where she had fallen. Melanie had seen people fall off at Clarebrook. If they were okay they usually jumped right up. Anna was still down.

Melanie felt nauseous. Seeing Anna fall off like that had made her remember her own fall. She hoped Anna wasn't badly hurt.

Naomi had stayed on Pirate but seemed to be having trouble settling him down. Pirate was still plunging and bucking, fighting Naomi for all he was worth. Naomi had a determined look on her face as she set her hands and pulled hard on the reins, wrestling for control. At last Pirate came around. He stopped resisting and slowed to a jog, and then a walk.

Ashleigh and Mr. McLean were still leaning over Anna. To Melanie's relief, Anna finally sat up and then slowly got to her feet. The girl's face was pale, but she managed to offer a reassuring smile. Ashleigh put an arm around Anna and helped her off the track. Anna bit her lip and kept her arms folded around her ribs as though they hurt.

Naomi had given Pirate to a hot walker, who led the horse away to cool him off. Mr. McLean was questioning her closely. Melanie could just make out what they were saying.

". . . looked like he went after the mare. Do you think that's what it was?" Mr. McLean asked.

Naomi wore a perplexed look. She shook her head. "I'm not sure. He seemed to be concentrating just fine. That buck just came out of nowhere—if it was a buck. And I'm not so sure he was playing. It seemed more like he suddenly tried to jump out of the way of something, but nothing was there." She shrugged. "I could be wrong." Naomi glanced back toward the finish line, where Pirate had acted up.

Melanie followed Naomi's gaze. She looked up and

down the track for something that could have spooked Pirate. A shadow from one of the oak trees around the outside of the training oval fell across the track near where he'd spooked. Had Pirate tried to jump the shadow?

Mr. McLean was shaking his head gravely. "I can't see any reason why the horse should have jumped like that. That was almost a bad accident and there was no excuse for it. Anna's very likely got some broken ribs. If that'd happened in a race—" He broke off and stared back at the finish line. "I just think we're going to have to geld him."

Naomi nodded sadly. "Maybe that's the best thing to do, if you really think he's behaving like a stallion. He's fast—that's for sure. If we geld him, maybe he'll keep his mind on racing instead of on the mares."

That night at dinner Melanie asked her aunt, "Are they going to geld Pirate?"

Ashleigh nodded. "It seems like that's the only thing to do. It's a shame, because his dam was a great-stakes horse. It'd be nice to be able to have him stand as a stallion one day. But all his speed isn't going to do him any good if he can't keep his mind on the race."

"It's a good thing," Christina said. "Poor Sterling might not have had her shoulder gashed open if he'd been gelded sooner. But why not just sell him?"

Melanie jerked to attention. Would they sell Pirate?

She'd heard them talking about some big horse auction coming up.

Ashleigh regarded her daughter. "We didn't just get rid of you that year you had so much trouble with your schoolwork," she said pointedly.

Christina scowled and Melanie smothered a grin.

"Pirate's got a lot of potential as a racehorse," Ashleigh went on. "It's our job to find the best conditions for him to perform at his best. If gelding him will help, it's worth a try."

"The only problem is, Pirate's entered in his first race next week. I hate to geld him right in the middle of the racing season, when he's just starting to run well," Mike said. "But on the other hand, we don't want to put him on the track with his attitude."

Listening to the conversation, Melanie bristled. She hated that word *attitude*. It had been applied to her many times, and not in a very nice way.

"Well, run him next week and see how he does. If he acts up, then we'll have to geld him. But maybe he'll be fine," Ashleigh pointed out. "It was too bad Anna got hurt this morning, but after all, we're not really sure what happened. Let's give him one more chance."

Melanie thought about the incident at the track. Something about it was bothering her. Suddenly she remembered the day she'd been watching Ian try to lead Pirate into the starting gate. Pirate had spooked and balked at the gate until Melanie led him in. But that was when the weather had turned cloudy, she remembered. Maybe Pirate had just been afraid of the shadow. This morning the finish was near the same spot.

"That's it!" Melanie said out loud.

10

"WHAT'S IT?" CHRISTINA ASKED.

"Pirate's afraid of shadows!" Melanie announced.

"What are you talking about?" Christina said.

"All the time he was causing so much trouble at the gate, there was a shadow across it. The sun went behind a cloud about the same time I led him into the gate. And this morning when he bumped into the other horse, there was a shadow at the same place!" Melanie explained. "I think maybe he tried to jump over it."

Ashleigh was looking at her. "You may have something there, Melanie," Ashleigh told her. "Hmm. I wonder if that was it." She glanced at Mike.

"If that's all it was, we could try him with blinkers," Mike suggested. "Maybe we don't need to geld him after all."

"What are blinkers?" Melanie asked.

"They cover part of the horse's eyes," Christina told her. "They keep the horse from seeing much except what's right ahead of him."

"Oh, like the carriage horses wear in New York," Melanie said.

"Exactly," Uncle Mike said. "Except that racing blinkers are attached to a hood over the horse's head, and there are many different kinds, depending on the problem you're having with the horse."

"Well, let's try the Australian blinkers on him tomorrow and see how he does," Ashleigh suggested. "Maybe that'll solve the problem."

"What are they?" Melanie asked.

"They're sort of like a window screen. They just soften everything in the horse's field of vision so that he won't see shadows and spook at them," Ashleigh explained. "You're a smart girl, Melanie," she said approvingly. "You may have just saved us a stallion."

Inside, Melanie was pleased that she might have figured out what was causing Pirate's problems on the track. But she was careful not to show it. She took a small bite of her salad.

"So Melanie, how do you like it here at Whitebrook so far?" her aunt asked her.

"It's okay," Melanie said. But the question reminded her of the conversations with her father and Aynslee. She put down her fork.

"And how's the shoulder feeling?"

113

"Fine," Melanie said.

"I think you get the sling off at the end of next week, right?" Ashleigh went on brightly.

"Yeah, I think so," Melanie said. Suddenly she was suspicious. Where was all this leading?

"Well, your uncle and I were talking, and here's what we think," Ashleigh proposed. She glanced across the table at Uncle Mike, who nodded his approval. "As soon as your sling comes off and you can use both arms, we'll put you in charge of one of the yearlings. You can have all the responsibility of caring for it, grooming it, training it—the whole thing."

"And if you do a good job, which I know you will, at the end of the summer it'll be your horse. How does that sound?" Uncle Mike put in.

Dumbfounded, Melanie looked back and forth from her aunt to her uncle, as if she were watching a tennis match. Did adults ever listen to a single thing kids said? Melanie wondered. Hadn't she made it perfectly clear that she wasn't going to ride horses anymore? And now they were trying to give her a yearling colt or filly. What were they thinking?

She was still going to be Pirate's groom, of course, but that was different. She was just helping out Mr. McLean. Melanie was about to tell them in no uncertain terms that she didn't want anything to do with any horse of any kind. But before she could say no, Christina spoke.

"You're giving her a horse?" Christina asked.

Melanie didn't miss the sharpness of the question, although Christina had spoken softly.

"Yes," Ashleigh said. "You've seen most of the yearlings by now. Haven't you, Mel? Is there one in particular you'd like to work with?" she asked.

Melanie heard her aunt's words, but she was watching Christina's face. The girl wore a look of disbelief.

Melanie was instantly defensive. Why wouldn't Christina want her to have a horse? She wondered if she could stomach taking care of a yearling all summer, just to get at Christina. But then she had an even better idea. Christina didn't care for Pirate. She was still miffed about the incident where Pirate gashed Sterling's shoulder. And Melanie was still angry at Christina for being so annoyingly correct all the time and for acting as though Sterling were a baby or something instead of just a horse. If she could get Uncle Mike and Aunt Ashleigh to give her Pirate for the summer, it would drive Christina nuts. But of course they weren't going to give her a full-grown three-year-old stallion. And even if they did, Melanie thought bitterly, she'd probably just end up losing him.

Melanie stood up and picked up her plate. "I'll keep working with Pirate since Mr. McLean needs me. But I'm not interested in owning a horse," she told them. "Excuse me." She took her plate to the sink and was about to go upstairs when her aunt stopped her.

"Wait a moment, please, Melanie."

Melanie turned around and waited for her aunt to go on.

"I've been meaning to talk to you about Pirate," Ashleigh said.

Melanie was instantly on guard. "What about him?"

"Well, another reason we'd like you to take over one of the yearlings is . . ." Aunt Ashleigh paused, then delivered the news. "We don't think you should be Pirate's groom anymore."

"What?" Melanie froze.

"It's just not a good idea," Ashleigh said. "Pirate's a lot of horse, even for an adult. You know all the problems we've had with him."

Mike agreed. "Your aunt's right, Mel. I know you're fond of Pirate, but he's not the kind of horse a kid should be handling. Pick one of the yearlings. They're littler and easier to take care of. And if you work with one, at the end of the summer you can look at him and say, 'I brought this horse along.' "

Melanie ignored the talk about the yearling. "I'm the one who finally got Pirate to go into the starting gate, you know," she said to her aunt and uncle. "Maybe it wasn't the shadow. Maybe it was me. And he's been doing great since I've been working with him. Ian says I have a way with him."

"Honey, it's great that you were able to help us out with Pirate, but that still doesn't make him an appropriate horse for you," Ashleigh said. "Especially now, when he's having some behavior problems."

"Behavior problems," Melanie echoed scornfully. Those were the exact words Mr. Howard had used to describe Melanie's conduct in school. Just because she didn't always go along with the crowd. What was wrong with being a little different? "Maybe it's not behavior *problems*," Melanie said. "Maybe he's just different."

"It's a problem if a horse leaps into the air and runs into other horses at forty miles an hour," Ashleigh observed dryly. "You saw what happened to Anna. She's got three cracked ribs and won't be able to ride for a good while."

"He's never done anything with me," Melanie tried. "Maybe it's just bad luck. And you said the blinkers would help," she reminded them.

Ashleigh sighed. "Melanie, you just have to understand. We're willing to let you work with a yearling, but under the circumstances I just don't think it's safe for you to be handling Pirate on your own all the time. Tomorrow we'll go pick one of the yearlings and he can be as good as yours. Or she," she added.

"No thank you," Melanie said. "Pirate's the only horse I'm interested in working with." She turned around and went upstairs. At the top of the stairs she paused. She could hear them talking downstairs.

". . . you think we'll ever get her to get back on a horse that way?" Uncle Mike was saying.

"I think it's a start," Aunt Ashleigh said. "If we can get her to care for a yearling, she'll come around. How

117

could anyone resist? Besides, it'll keep her too busy to get into any trouble."

So that was it. They all had this big plan to get her riding again and make sure she had plenty of barn chores to do so that she wouldn't mess up anything. Melanie couldn't believe they thought she was that dumb.

"I can't believe you're actually going to give her a horse." That was Christina's voice. Melanie silently stepped down a couple of stairs so that she could hear her cousin better.

"Why, Chris? Your cousin's been through some bad times—losing her mom when she was little, having her dad away most of the time," Uncle Mike said. "We want to help her out if we can."

"Oh yeah. She has it so rough," Christina said.

"Christina, why are you being so hard on her?" Ashleigh asked.

"You know what she did to me?" Christina said. "When we were in New York this spring and we went riding at that stable, she put me on the nastiest horse in the barn. She tried to get me hurt," Christina said.

"Chrissy, that can't be true," Mike objected.

"It is true, Dad," Christina insisted. "And *please* don't call me Chrissy. You know I hate it."

"Sorry. Christina. But I doubt Melanie would try to get you hurt," Mike said.

"Well, she did," Christina told him. "She had them put me on this horse that bucks and bolts like crazy. I know—I heard two women talking about him. And even the woman at the front desk wasn't sure I should ride him. Then Melanie started telling her what a great rider I was and all."

"Well, that sounds like a compliment to me," Ashleigh commented. "But if you doubted whether you could ride the horse, why didn't you refuse to get on him?"

"I didn't doubt that I could ride him," Christina said.

"And did he act that badly?"

"Horrible," Christina said. "He bucked and ran away with me, even worse than my pony used to."

"And did you ride through it okay?"

"Of course I did," Christina said.

"Well, then, what was the problem?" Ashleigh wanted to know. "Melanie thought you were a good rider. You thought you could ride the horse, and you did."

Alone in the dark at the top of the stairs, Melanie remembered the incident Christina was talking about and felt a tiny stab of guilt. She had half hoped that Kenwood, the horse in question, would buck Christina off. But she really hadn't meant her any harm. And she had ended up admiring Christina's riding instead.

"I still don't think you should just give her a horse," Christina was saying.

"You keep saying that," Uncle Mike said. "Why not?"

"Because she's a *horse killer*," Christina hissed. "Don't you remember what she did to that horse in New York?"

11

MELANIE HAD HEARD ALL SHE COULD STAND. SHE GOT UP AND stumbled down the hall to her room. It was true. It was all true. Milky Way was gone and there was no way she could make up for his death. Even though she hadn't meant any harm, it had happened and it was all her fault, and the horrible feeling it gave her was never going to go away, not ever. She could push it down and hide it for a while, but it would always be there and there was nothing she could do about it.

And what if her cousin was right? All the accidents with Pirate had happened when Melanie was around. Maybe she had caused them somehow. Maybe she was bad luck for horses.

As hard as she'd tried not to fall in love with Pirate, she knew she had, anyway. It hurt that she wasn't going to be allowed to handle him anymore. But maybe it was

120

for the best. Maybe if she stayed away from him, no more accidents would happen.

"I won't go near him anymore. And I won't love him anymore," she whispered fiercely. "And then I can't hurt him and I can't lose him."

Melanie couldn't speak to Christina after that night. She withdrew into stony silence, only showing up for meals and sometimes going without eating when she couldn't bear the thought of her aunt and uncle making cheerful conversation while she sat across from her cousin's accusing gaze.

She still listened for news about Pirate's progress, although she wouldn't go near him. And everything she heard sounded good. They tried the colt with the special blinkers, and so far there had been no more incidents, so he was registered to run with them.

"Pirate's going in his first race this Saturday," Aunt Ashleigh told her a few days later.

"I know," Melanie said. Hadn't she spent a whole week as his groom, helping him get ready for the race?

"Would you like to come and see him run?"

"No thanks," Melanie said. She took her sketchbook and went outside.

On the day of Pirate's race, Uncle Mike came upstairs and found Melanie in her room. He tapped on the door, which was open, and waited.

Melanie was sitting at the little desk. She had started

to write a letter to her dad, but it had turned into a drawing of a galloping horse. "Come in," she said. She heard the wood floor creak as he stepped into the room, but she didn't turn around.

"Pirate's running at Keeneland today," Uncle Mike told her. "I thought maybe you'd like to come and see him run."

"No thanks," Melanie said, just as she'd said when her aunt invited her. She'd made up her mind to stay away from horses once and for all.

"Mel, it's really exciting, watching a race. Especially when you have a favorite," he tried. "I know you'll have a great time."

"I don't have any favorites," Melanie told him. She began to color the horse black.

He sighed. "I've got to get out to the track. We have a few other horses running today besides Pirate. Ashleigh and Christina have already gone. Sure you don't want to come?"

"I'm sure," Melanie said, though deep down she badly wanted to go.

"Okay, then," he said. "See you later."

"Bye." Melanie heard the floor creak as he left the room. She put down the pen and folded her arms on the desk, resting her chin on them dejectedly. If she were at home, she would've boiled some Kool-Aid and streaked her hair with it to make herself feel better. But she hadn't bothered to do that since she came to Kentucky, and now she realized she didn't really want to. Dying her hair was just a way of distracting herself when she felt sad or lonely or angry. It worked for a little while, but not really for long.

The Reeses came back from Keeneland happy with the way the horses had performed. Saturday Affair had won a big-stakes race and two of the colts had done well in maiden races. Best of all, Pirate had won his first race by many lengths.

"Oh, that's good," Melanie said politely when they told her about the race. But inside she was glad. *Good for you, Pirate Treasure,* she thought. *I knew you were a winner.*

The following week Pirate won an allowance race for three-year-olds. Melanie had wandered over to the training barn as the horses were getting back from the race.

"How'd you do with Pirate?" Anna called to Naomi as she climbed out of the truck. Anna had already started riding again, though her ribs were still healing.

"He set a track record!" Naomi said excitedly to Anna. "The horse is just amazing! He's a front-runner all the way and he never fades! Anna, it's such a different ride with nobody in front of you the whole way," Naomi told her.

Melanie was delighted that Pirate was doing so well. She hung back, listening to Anna and Naomi talk about riding racehorses. For the first time she allowed herself to imagine what it would feel like to be on a horse again, galloping up a grassy hill. Wistfully she remembered the feel of Pirate's silky black coat under her hands. She wished she could feel it again, but obviously she had been right—the horse was doing better without her around.

On the day Melanie was scheduled to get the sling off her arm, Uncle Mike drove her to the doctor's office. The X ray showed that the shoulder had healed fine.

"How does it feel?" Uncle Mike asked her.

"Pretty good," Melanie said, testing it gently. It was stiff but not too sore anymore.

"Great," Uncle Mike said. "Listen, I've just got to take care of some business out at Keeneland. I hope you don't mind coming along with me."

"Whatever," Melanie said. She really didn't care. It was just as easy to spend the morning riding around with her uncle as it was to spend it avoiding her cousin. She slumped down in the cab of the truck and closed her eyes.

Melanie woke up when the truck stopped. She opened her eyes and looked over at her uncle.

"Have a nice nap?" he said, smiling.

Melanie sat up slowly. "Where are we?" she asked.

"I told you I had business at Keeneland," Uncle Mike said, opening the door of the truck. "Lock it," he said to Melanie.

Melanie got out and followed her uncle through a

large parking lot. "What is this place, anyway?" she asked him.

He gave her a glance. "Keeneland Race Track," he told her.

Melanie stopped. When her uncle said he had business at Keeneland, she hadn't imagined he meant the racetrack. Pirate Treasure was racing that day at Keeneland, she knew.

"What are you bringing me here for?" Melanie asked.

"I have a horse running here today," Uncle Mike said. "And I know he's a favorite of yours. I think it's time you saw him run."

"I can't be near him," Melanie protested. "I can't be around horses anymore. Don't you understand? It's— it's like, whenever I start to care about a horse, something bad happens. At first I was so mad that you said I couldn't be Pirate's groom anymore, but I know it's better that way. He's better off without me around. Please don't make me do this," Melanie begged.

Uncle Mike put his hands on Melanie's shoulders. "Melanie, listen. You've punished yourself enough, okay? Ashleigh and I thought it wasn't safe for you to be around Pirate, but that was because of him, not you. I know you care about the horse and I think you should see him run. He's doing great, and when you see I think you'll be so proud of him."

Melanie couldn't speak. She wanted to see Pirate run more than anything, but she was so afraid that she would see something bad happen.

"Life goes on, Melanie," Uncle Mike said softly. "I know you've had it rough, but things are going to be better now."

Full of hope and just as full of doubt, Melanie let her uncle lead her into the grandstand to watch Pirate Treasure's race.

Pirate was entered in an allowance race for three-year-olds and up. The purse was twenty thousand dollars. When it was actually post time, Melanie was almost frantic. I shouldn't be here, she kept thinking. Something bad is going to happen. I shouldn't be here.

Melanie's aunt and uncle had box seats, but Melanie hadn't wanted to sit with them. Instead she stood next to Ian down by the rail. She watched anxiously as one by one the horses went into the starting gate. Pirate walked right in without seeming to care. "Good," Melanie whispered. "Good boy."

Then before she knew it, the start bell sounded. "Theeeeey're off!" the announcer chanted.

Pirate was out of the gate and up front the minute it opened. Melanie stood in awe, watching the powerful horse churn down the track. They had started on the far side and seemed so far away they were like toy horses and riders moving down the track.

Then they were rounding the turn. Pirate was still in the lead, but another horse was closing on him. As they came down the homestretch, Pirate held the lead by a neck, but the little bay mare was stretching her stride, gaining on him inch by inch. The rest of the field was far behind.

"Come on, Pirate," Melanie said. "You can do it." She had two sets of fingers crossed on each hand. Then she crossed the crossed fingers. "Go, go, go, go, go," she chanted.

Pirate went. He suddenly seemed to kick in and run even harder. Melanie watched as they flashed past. The mare was still holding her own beside him, but she had made her move and didn't seem to have anything else left in her. Naomi hadn't touched her stick yet. Pirate blazed past the finish wire a length ahead of the mare.

"All right, Pirate!" Melanie cheered.

"Pirate Treasure does it again," Ian said with a smile.

Suddenly there was a gasp from the crowd. Melanie looked for Pirate and felt her heart begin to pound. The horse wasn't slowing. He was still going hard toward the next turn. The rest of the field had slowed up, all except the mare. She was still running beside Pirate, on his outside. It seemed as though the two horses thought the race wasn't over yet.

"Come on, Naomi, pull up," Ian said. His face showed concern, but he just stood calmly watching to see what would happen.

"What's the matter?" Melanie asked. "Why aren't they stopping?"

"Well, it looks like we've got a couple of runaways,"

Ian told her. "Don't worry, though. The outriders will stop them."

Melanie looked. Two of the pony riders who accompanied horses to the gate were galloping down after the runaways. Soon Melanie saw what they were doing— they were trying to split up the two racehorses and pin them against the inside rail, forcing them to stop. But just as they reached Pirate and the mare, Pirate lunged toward the outside. He slammed into the mare's shoulder, just as he had done to Faith that day in his workout.

"Oh no," Melanie said.

The mare fell as Pirate rammed her. Pirate kept going toward the outside rail and crashed right through it. This time Naomi couldn't stay on. She fell hard on the other side of the fence. Pirate ran for a few more strides, then stopped. He stood swinging his head from side to side, looking bewildered. Even from as far away as she was, Melanie could see the flash of blood, bright red against his deep black chest.

12

Ian swore softly. "Come on," he said to Melanie. He took her left hand and started to pull her through the crowd.

"Oh no! Oh no!" Melanie moaned. "Not again, please."

"Come on, Melanie. Pull yourself together," Ian said sharply. "I need your help out there, please."

"It's all my fault," Melanie cried. "I shouldn't be here. I should never have come. It's all my fault."

"Nonsense. You had nothing to do with it," Ian said, pulling her through the crowd. "The horse did it to himself. But now you can do something. You can help him! Come on."

Melanie was in agony. She thought her heart was going to pop right out of her chest. But something in Ian's tone made her hold herself together. Somehow she

129

followed Ian down the track to the hole in the fence where Pirate had gone through.

Somehow Melanie got to Pirate. She led him to the trailer and held him and soothed him while the vet was called. Lorelei Lanum, or "Dr. L" as she was known, arrived within minutes and began stitching up the huge rip in Pirate's chest where the jagged edge of the rail had stabbed him. Melanie had never seen so much blood come from one cut.

"Keep him on stall rest for a week, with just hand walking to keep him from getting stiff," Dr. L. ordered when she had finished stitching the horse. Dr. L. had wavy brown hair and pretty blue-green eyes. She was known for being calm and caring with her big patients. She patted Pirate's neck. "Poor old man," she said softly. "You're going to be sore for a while." She also prescribed some antibiotics and some medication known as "bute," which Melanie knew was like aspirin for horses.

"How's the jockey?" Dr. Lanum asked Ian.

He frowned. "Ashleigh just called and said they think she has a concussion and maybe a cracked wrist. They're keeping her overnight for observation."

"That's too bad," Dr. L. said. "How's the other one?"

"The horse pulled a tendon," Ian said. "But the jockey's okay. They're lucky that's all that happened. The way Pirate slammed into that horse . . ." His voice trailed off and he seemed to be thinking deeply. Then he sighed. "Lorelei, I'll have to confirm this with Mike and Ashleigh, but we discussed it already. I think we ought to geld this horse before he causes any more trouble. Can you come out and do it next week?"

"Sure," Dr. Lanum said. "Just give him a few days to get over the shock and I'll take care of it."

A few hours later it was all over. Melanie saw that Pirate was safely back in his stall at Whitebrook. Dazed, she walked out of the barn and back up to the house. Somehow she found her way upstairs and into the attic. All through the ordeal of watching Pirate's race end in tragedy, and all the time she had helped hold him and talked to him while Dr. L. stitched his wound, Melanie had remained calm. But now she could feel the tears burning the backs of her eyes. It was a relief to let them come. She gazed out the window across the pasture toward the training barn where she knew Pirate was standing in his stall, in pain from his injury. And now they were going to geld him. There would never be any foals by Pirate Treasure. "I'm sorry, Pirate," Melanie whispered. "I should have stayed away. It's all my fault. I know it is. I'm just bad luck."

"No, it's not," someone said.

Melanie jumped. She had thought she was alone in the attic, but when she turned around she saw Christina. "I didn't know you were here," Melanie said.

"I just came up," Christina said.

"How come I didn't hear you?" Melanie asked.

"I guess you were too busy blaming yourself," Christina suggested. "Besides, I know where the creaky spots are on the stairs. I step around them."

"What do you want?" Melanie said. She swiped at her wet face with her shirttail, which was still splotched with Pirate's blood.

"Well, I wanted to be alone for a while," Christina said. "This is where I come when I want to hide out."

"Looks like we had the same idea," Melanie said. "I'll leave," she said, starting for the stairs.

"No, it's okay. Stay," Christina said.

Melanie hesitated. "Why?"

"Listen, what happened to Pirate? It's not your fault," Christina said. "Mom told me about it."

"I shouldn't have been there. I just shouldn't have been there," Melanie said, feeling the tears threaten to come again. "Everything I do turns out wrong. I'm bad luck, especially for horses."

"No, you're not," Christina said. "That day when Pirate struck at Sterling, that wasn't your fault, either. I was just upset. I shouldn't have blamed you."

"Why not? I'm a horse killer, remember?" Melanie said bitterly.

Christina blushed. "I didn't mean that," she said. "It was wrong of me to say that. I know you didn't mean for the horse to get hurt."

"Of course I didn't mean it," Melanie said furiously. "But he did. Not just hurt. He got killed. And now Pirate's hurt, too. And it's all because of me." The tears began to flow down her cheeks again, but this time she did nothing to stop them.

"Mel, stop punishing yourself," Christina said gently.

"You can't do anything about that horse in New York, but Pirate needs you. He loves you—everybody can see it."

"I'm afraid," Melanie sobbed. "I'm afraid to go near him. What if he dies, too? What if he dies and it's all because of me? I couldn't stand it. I just couldn't stand to lose him, too."

Christina went over and stood next to Melanie. Melanie felt her cousin slowly put an arm around her shoulders. She stiffened at first. It seemed as though it had been such a long time since she'd felt anyone touch her in a caring way. But then she let Christina keep her arm there, and she was glad.

"Hey," Christina said. "Some horses just click with certain people—you know that. Pirate likes you. And right now, he really needs you. You're not going to kill him. But you could help him get better."

"Yeah?" Melanie asked, looking her cousin in the eye for the first time in weeks. She was surprised to see that the look in Christina's hazel eyes was friendly and concerned.

"Yeah," Christina said.

Dr. Lanum came the next week and gelded Pirate. Then he was put on turnout until all his stitches healed. Melanie didn't want to go near him, but one day Christina convinced her to just come to the paddock and visit him. Reluctantly, Melanie agreed.

She hadn't seen Pirate since the day of the accident. When Christina led her to the field where he was turned out every day, she hardly recognized him. The once majestic horse looked thin and bedraggled. There was an ugly jagged scar on his chest where the stitches had been. And he moved stiffly, like a much older horse.

"Poor Pirate," Melanie said. Her eyes filled with tears again. "Doesn't anybody care about him?" she asked Christina.

Christina told her, "He can't start back in training yet. Ian says he doesn't want to push him. Maybe next year he'll make a comeback."

"But he looks so sad," Melanie said. "Look at him."

"Maybe you should come visit him more often," Christina pointed out. "Look—he's happy to see you."

The girls had climbed over the fence and walked over to Pirate. When he heard Melanie's voice, he picked up his ears and turned his head toward her. Then he found a strand of her hair and nibbled at it.

"Poor old Pirate," Melanie crooned, stroking his neck.

After that, Melanie visited the horse every day. She brought him carrots and apples but had to coax him to eat. He was listless and didn't seem interested in anything. Melanie worried about him.

Then early one morning she was hand walking him around the grounds. She wandered over near the training oval, just as a group of horses made a start out of the gate. When Pirate heard the pounding hooves, his head snapped up and he began turning it from side to side, as if he were looking for the race. "Where's the finish line?" his expression seemed to say. "Point me at it!"

"So that's it," Melanie said. "You miss the race track!"

Pirate tossed his head proudly, as if she had guessed the answer. He began to prance in place as he had on the way to his workouts, before his injury. But as soon as Melanie led him away, his head began to droop again and he resumed his stiff-legged walk. When she had put Pirate back in his paddock, Melanie went to find Ian.

He listened to her description of Pirate's behavior. Then he said, "I believe you, Melanie. But I just don't have time to fool with him right now. He's never going to come back this season and I don't see any reason to rush it. You can hand walk him by the track all you want, if you think it helps. He could even go under saddle by now."

"You mean he could be ridden?" she asked.

"Sure," Ian said. "I just don't have any reason to work the horse right now. I'd put somebody on him just to keep him in shape, but I don't have a spare exercise rider right now," Ian said.

It wasn't until later that it occurred to Melanie that she could be the rider herself. In spite of her vow never to ride again, she knew that Pirate needed her. Christina was right. It was too late to save Milky Way. But Melanie could help save Pirate. She put her plan into action the following morning.

It was easy to slip into the tack room when everyone was busy and borrow a bridle. She didn't need a saddle—not yet, anyway. Melanie hung the bridle over her shoulder, and taking a carrot, went out to Pirate where he was turned out in the field. A few moments later she had slipped the bit into his mouth and fastened the bridle on his head.

"Okay, Pirate. Let's do it," she said. She led him to the fence and climbed up it.

Pirate stood calmly beside her. She stared at his shiny black back and began to tremble. She was terrified.

She hesitated, staring at the horse. Was she taking a terrible chance riding him? Then she told herself it didn't matter. Pirate's life was wrecked, just as much as Melanie's was. Things couldn't get much worse for either one of them.

Melanie knew if she didn't get on Pirate, she would never get on any other horse. She and Pirate had both been through terrible accidents. Melanie was sure Pirate would understand her.

Her heart was beating fast as she gathered up the reins and prepared to mount up. Then, just the way she made up her mind to jump into a cold pool, she slipped a leg over his back and scrambled on.

Pirate didn't move. He stood calmly, waiting for Melanie to tell him what to do. For a moment Melanie didn't move, either. Then she adjusted the reins and carefully squeezed Pirate into a walk with her legs.

Melanie hadn't been on a horse since the night she fell off Milky Way. It all came back to her now, but in a different way. Milky Way's face was clear in her mind, and Pirate's body was firm underneath her and suddenly she felt calm and strong. She knew that there was a way to make up for Milky Way's death and this was it. She could ride Pirate—she could help Pirate recover by riding him. The thought made Melanie feel almost happy again for the first time in a very long time.

After that, she slipped out into the field and rode Pirate every morning. At first Melanie just walked him around. She didn't want to push him. But one day he seemed to want to trot, so she let him. After that, she trotted around the field every day.

She remembered that he might spook at shadows, so she avoided them, but one day she trotted him right into the shadow of a cedar bush before she'd realized it. But Pirate didn't react at all. Melanie guessed maybe he'd gotten over his fear of shadows.

Pirate was still thin and seemed depressed, except when Melanie slipped the bridle on him. Then he perked up and moved willingly, slowly working the stiffness out of his muscles. "Don't worry, Pirate," Melanie said. "One day you're going to race again." She hand walked him by the training oval every day and was glad to see that he always seemed to come alive again whenever he was near the other racehorses.

After a while she was cantering him as well. Melanie felt her own confidence and strength coming back as Pirate's muscles began to build up. She was still riding him bareback, with just a bridle, but she found she was comfortable that way. Pirate's smooth back and easy strides made it simple. She thought about telling Ian but decided to wait a while. Riding Pirate was the first thing that had made her feel truly happy again. She wanted to keep it to herself for a little while longer.

One day Melanie was cantering around the field. The trunk of a tree that had fallen a few years before still lay in the middle of the field. Melanie hadn't jumped in a long time, but suddenly she felt the urge. She turned Pirate and pointed him toward the log.

Pirate cantered smoothly along. Just as they reached the spot where he should take off, Melanie bent forward into jumping position and grabbed a handful of Pirate's mane, just to be sure she stayed on.

She should have felt the jump then—the brief but pleasant sensation of sailing through the air over the back of a horse and the landing on the other side. Instead she felt Pirate trip over the log as if he had no idea it were there. Both of them somersaulted and fell side by side on the grass on the other side of the log.

Pirate leaped to his feet and began looking wildly left and right. Melanie got up just as quickly. The ground was soft. She wasn't hurt, but she was worried that Pirate was.

"It's okay, boy," she said, catching him by the reins. He seemed agitated and stepped toward her, bumping right into her and nearly knocking her down.

"What's the matter, Pirate?" she asked, puzzled. "Didn't you see that log?"

Suddenly it dawned on Melanie. He hadn't seen it. And he hadn't seen Faith when he bumped her in training that day. And he hadn't seen the mare at Keeneland, or the rail before he crashed through it.

Pirate had calmed down. Melanie waved her hand right by the horse's left eye. No reaction. Then she tried the right. Pirate just stood, sniffing the air. She picked up a stick and waved it before both eyes. Pirate didn't budge. He didn't see her hand or the stick. And he hadn't spooked at the shadow that day because he hadn't seen that, either. Pirate couldn't see anything at all. He was blind.

When Melanie told Ian her theory, he agreed to have Pirate's vision checked. Ashleigh and Mike came into the barn to hear what the vet would say. Dr. Lanum confirmed Melanie's guess. "He's got moon blindness," Dr. L. told them. "It's a degenerative eye disease. Looks like it came on pretty quickly. Probably he could see shadows for a while, and then he just lost it completely."

"That explains why he jumped at the shadow that day in training," Ian mused.

"And why he settled down temporarily with the Australian blinkers," Ashleigh said. "Except that with the blinkers on, he was probably nearly blind."

"Can he race again?" Melanie wanted to know.

Mike shook his head. "I'm afraid not. Pirate's racing days are over."

"What will you do with him then?" Melanie asked.

Ian sighed. "Well, we haven't got much use for a blind horse around here. Maybe we can find him a paddock somewhere and just retire him."

"But he'll be so unhappy," Melanie protested. "He still loves the track, even though he can't race. You've seen how happy he is when I hand walk him there."

"That's true, Melanie. But the horse is blind. What can we do?" Ian said gently. "They won't let a blind horse race. He'd be a danger to himself and the other horses."

"Why not make him a pony horse?" Dr. L. suggested.

"What do you mean?" Melanie asked.

"Pony horses are the horses we use to accompany the racehorses to the gate," Ashleigh said.

"Oh," Melanie said. She had seen them at Keeneland.

"I've known plenty of good ponies that were blind in one eye or both," Dr. L. went on. "They're usually the best ones because they never spook at anything."

"But who's going to ride him?" Ian asked.

"Melanie is," Christina said. She had just come into the barn leading Sterling.

"Melanie doesn't ride anymore. Remember?" Mike said gently.

"Yes she does," Christina said. "She's been riding Pirate every morning. I've been watching her."

"Me too," Kevin chimed. He was right behind Christina with Jasper.

"Is that true, Melanie?" Ashleigh asked.

Melanie stared at Ashleigh and again felt as though Ashleigh could see straight through her with those penetrating eyes. Melanie blushed.

"Yeah, it's true. I've been riding him for a few weeks. So am I going to get in trouble? Are you going to send me home now or what?" she said, placing her hands on her hips and staring around at them defiantly. "Nobody cared about him but me," she went on. "So I just did it, okay? It seemed to make him happy. . . ." She felt her defiant tone waver. "I just wanted him to be happy," she said. "I wasn't trying to cause trouble." She looked around, trying to figure out why no one was saying anything. Then she realized that Ashleigh was smiling.

"Nobody's sending you anywhere, Melanie, unless you want to go. And we're not sending Pirate anywhere, either, as long as you're willing to take care of him," Ashleigh promised.

"Pirate's yours," Mike agreed.

"You deserve him," Christina added.

"I've got a little proposal for you," Ian said. "I'm a little short staffed at the moment. How'd you like to be my number one pony girl?"

"Only you'll have to hang around this place a while longer," Mike said.

Melanie felt a small smile begin at the corner of her mouth and slowly spread into a grin. She stepped toward Pirate. "Do you want me to stay, Pirate?" she asked the horse.

Pirate Treasure lowered his head and sniffed at Melanie. When he realized who it was, he found a strand of her hair and lipped it playfully. Then he pushed his big head into her chest, as if he'd found his favorite place to be. Melanie didn't often feel safe enough with people to trust them with her deepest feelings. But at that moment, she knew, she trusted this horse. And he trusted her.

"How could I leave him?" she said softly.

"Look's like you're going to be here for a while then, Mel," Kevin said. "You better make yourself at home."

Suddenly New York seemed like a place she'd visited in a dream. Whitebrook was real. There were no housekeepers, or chauffeurs, or fancy schools with uniforms. Just people who seemed to care about horses, and about her. She reached up and put her arms around Pirate's massive head. "I am at home," Melanie said. And she felt it was true.

Look for the next exciting
Thoroughbred adventure,

STERLING'S SECOND CHANCE

Coming Soon from HarperPaperbacks

"JUMP THAT OUTSIDE LINE AGAIN, CHRISTINA, BUT THIS time put six strides between the fences instead of five. Then come around and jump the liverpool."

Christina Reese gave her riding instructor, Mona Gardener, a nod that meant she understood. She tucked a stray lock of her strawberry blond hair behind her ear. Then she shortened her reins and urged her four-year-old Thoroughbred mare into a trot. "Did you hear that, Sterling?" Christina said to the horse. "You've got to slow down and listen to me."

Sterling Dream tossed her head and let out a snort. Her dapple gray coat was darkened with sweat even though it was early morning and still fairly cool. The summer sun glinted on the mare's muscled haunches as she cantered, and flashed in the silver streaks of her black mane and tail.

"That's it," Mona said, nodding approvingly as Christina moved Sterling out of the circle and headed toward the two jumps. Tall, slim Mona stood still near the center of the arena, her hands on her hips. Her head turned slightly as she watched Christina canter by. Christina could feel Mona's clear gray eyes taking in every detail of her form as she rode. "That's your pace," Mona encouraged. "Now just hold her there. Don't let her speed up."

Christina pushed her heels down and lifted her chin, trying to seem confident to Mona and to her horse, but inside she didn't feel very confident at all.

"Easy, girl," she murmured to the horse as she came closer and closer to the first jump. Sterling had been coming along beautifully ever since Christina had gotten her in a claiming race at Belmont Park racetrack in the spring. With Mona's guidance, they'd been training for a two-day event coming up at a neighboring farm called Foxwood Acres. The event included a novice horse trial on the first day for teams of horses and riders who were just starting out in combined training. The three riders on each team would be individually tested in dressage and on a cross-country jump course. Then their scores would be combined for the overall team score.

Christina wasn't worried about the dressage test. She and Sterling had been practicing the training-level test for weeks. Christina knew the moves by heart, and she thought by now Sterling must know them, too, because the mare seemed to know what cue Christina was going to give her even before she gave it. It was the jumping that Christina was worried about.

She had always thought jumping was the best thing about riding, and it had always been easy for her. She was as comfortable jumping a horse over a three-foot fence as she was asleep in her own bed. Just when she'd been ready to move on to jumping higher fences, she'd found Sterling.

At first Sterling had seemed to love jumping as much as Christina. But lately the mare had been rushing the fences. And during the past week she had even run out a couple of times, ducking to the side at the last second instead of jumping. Christina had nearly fallen off both times because she hadn't expected it. She glanced over at the liverpool, a four-foot-wide rectangle of water with a low rail set across the middle of it to encourage the horse to clear it. In the cross-country course at Foxwood there was a water ditch. Christina had been trying to practice jumping the liverpool to get Sterling ready for it. But now she was having trouble with plain old verticals, and so far she hadn't even gotten Sterling to go near the water. With the event so close, Christina was beginning to really worry. Why had Sterling suddenly become difficult over fences?

With a final hopeful glance at Mona, Christina found herself facing the first jump, a vertical made of two rails painted green. The jump was only two and a half feet high. Christina had been schooling over jumps a foot higher, so it should have been easy for her. But the two-and-a-half-foot fence seemed to loom as high as a four-foot oxer. Christina could feel butterflies stir in her stomach with every stride as they cantered toward the jump.

"That's it, that's it," Mona said encouragingly. "Now just be consistent, Chris. If you stay exactly the same, she'll stay the same."

Christina heard Mona's words, but her eyes were fixed over the top rail of the fence. From long experience she bent forward into two-point position, ready to jump, and prepared herself to feel the thrust as Sterling launched her powerful body into the air to clear the fence.

She should have felt the wonderful, soaring sensation as the horse pushed off with her hind-quarters and became airborne in a soundless moment of perfect flight. She should have felt the momentary pressure in her legs and heels as she held herself steady on the landing after the jump, and then, like clockwork, the rhythmic canter away as she headed for the next jump.

But what Christina felt instead was the unpleasant sensation of being thrown forward over her horse's right shoulder as the mare stopped and ducked to the left to avoid jumping the fence. Christina found herself almost lying on Sterling's neck, hanging on with all her might as she struggled to get herself centered over the horse again. She would have fallen off, except that she had yanked on one of the reins as she pitched forward. Sterling's head had shot up in protest, but it had also kept Christina from going completely over and off.

"Pick your head up, Chris, and settle yourself back into the saddle." Out of habit, Christina obeyed Mona's calm command, and though she hadn't thought she could move, she did manage to push herself back and find the saddle again.

Sterling had been trotting swiftly toward the gate that led out of the arena. She stopped when she reached it and looked around expectantly, as if she thought someone should appear and open it for her. Mona laughed.

"Well, Princess, sorry your attendants aren't here to open the palace gates for you," she joked as she walked over to Sterling and put a hand on the reins.

Ordinarily Christina would have laughed, too. Mona was her mother's best friend, and Christina had been taking lessons from her since she was four years old. One of the best things about Mona's teaching was that she was good at getting students to laugh at their mistakes. Mona never yelled, the way Christina had seen some instructors yell at their students; she was the best riding instructor in the world, as far as Christina was concerned.

But right then Christina forgot all that. She was

angry—angry at Sterling for running out at the jump, angry at Mona for joking about it, and most of all angry at herself for not being able to get Sterling over a little vertical without almost falling off. She hadn't even made it to the liverpool, which was the most difficult of the three fences. She stared fiercely at Sterling's withers while she impatiently stabbed at the stirrups with her feet, and she grew angrier still as she kept missing the left one.

Mona was holding Sterling's reins to steady the horse while Christina got herself together. She watched Christina trying to find the stirrup, and finally she held it steady in front of her foot. "Hey, what's the matter? You okay, Chris?" Mona was looking at Christina with concern.

"It's not funny!" Christina snapped. "Why are you laughing at me?"

Mona cocked her head, her eyes narrowing as she scrutinized Christina. "I'm not laughing at you," she said quietly. "You know that. Why are you so upset?"

"I'm not upset," Christina said through clenched teeth. She shortened the reins and turned Sterling away from the gate. The mare had been standing relaxed, but now her head went up again and her ears began to flick forward and back nervously. Christina felt the horse break into an antsy jog, and she shortened the reins more and pulled impatiently on them. Sterling walked, but Christina could feel that the mare wanted to move out. She gripped the reins hard with her hands, both to hold the mare at a walk and to keep her hands from trembling.

"Well, then, are you ready to try it again?" Mona asked.

Christina nodded. She wasn't ready at all. But she knew she had to make Sterling jump the fence.

ALLISON ESTES grew up in Oxford, Mississippi. She first sat on a horse when she was four years old, got a pony when she was ten, and has been riding horses ever since. Ms. Estes lives in New York City and works as a trainer at Claremont Riding Academy. She plays on four softball teams and, between games, has written over a dozen other books for young readers.

THOROUGHBRED

created by Joanna Campbell

Read all the books in the Thoroughbred series and experience the thrill of riding and racing, along with Ashleigh Griffen, Samantha McLean, Cindy McLean, and their beloved horses.